LOVE UNDER TWO BENEDICTS

Lusty, Texas 1

Cara Covington

MENAGE EVERLASTING

Siren Publishing, Inc.
www.SirenPublishing.com

A SIREN PUBLISHING BOOK
IMPRINT: Ménage Everlasting

LOVE UNDER TWO BENEDICTS
Copyright © 2010 by Cara Covington

ISBN-10: 1-61034-143-0
ISBN-13: 978-1-61034-143-1

First Printing: November 2010

Cover design by *Les Byerley*
All art and logo copyright © 2010 by Siren Publishing, Inc.

Printed in the U.S.A.

PUBLISHER
Siren Publishing, Inc.
www.SirenPublishing.com

LOVE UNDER TWO BENEDICTS

Lusty, Texas 1

CARA COVINGTON

Chapter 1

"I have no intention of being the bone you and your brother fight over, Deputy Benedict. So you can just take these flowers back, and you can both stop whatever game the two of you have been playing with me." Kelsey Madison quickly looked around her restaurant, Lusty Appetites, to ensure no one else happened to catch the slight snip in her tone.

No one seemed to be paying them any mind at all. *Good.* She was glad she'd decided to say something at last. She'd put it as plainly as she could. Everything she'd ever read or heard about Texas men suggested they appreciated plain talking.

It had never seemed to be a problem between her and Philip. She'd met him in college, a sweet, gentle man from Austin, Texas, who'd decided he wanted to take his schooling in Pennsylvania. They'd fallen in love at first sight and had married before they'd graduated.

Philip is gone. Stop thinking about him.

Kelsey blinked. For one moment, she thought she saw sympathy cross Matthew Benedict's face. That must have been a trick of the lighting because the expression he wore now was one of sly teasing.

"Now, Miss Kelsey, you must know by now that, while my brother and I would love for you to be the bone we nibbled on between us, we certainly would never fight over you. That's why we've both been wooing you. It's the Benedict way."

Kelsey blinked because what he'd just said implied that he and his brother, Steven…

Her eyes widened as that thought grew. Matthew nodded as if he could read her mind. He smiled at her when she knew the look on her face had to be one of absolute disbelief.

At this moment, it didn't matter that Matthew and his brother were the first men in five years to stir her juices and prime her pump. *That* was her secret. What he'd just implied was the last thing she'd ever expected to hear.

"You…you and your brother want to *share* me? Are you *crazy?*" She immediately hunched her shoulders and gave the restaurant another quick scan. Shock must have made her believe she'd shouted that last question instead of whispering as she intended because, again, no one seemed to be paying them any attention whatsoever.

Matthew's grin slowly disappeared. He tilted his head to one side. "Susie said you'd been up to the big house for dinner a few times since you'd come to town."

Kelsey couldn't follow his line of reasoning. She furrowed her brow. "What does my being a guest of your sister and your family for dinner have to do with you and Steven *sharing* me?"

Matthew raised one eyebrow, and in that moment, he looked every inch the tall, arrogant Texan. Of course, maybe it couldn't be considered arrogance when he was one of the two most handsome, potently masculine men in town.

Okay, Kels, that was a totally inappropriate thought. You're supposed to be discouraging these two Lotharios, not thinking about how they rev your engine.

Kelsey chased that thought out of her mind, or tried to. Much to her annoyance, it settled right down in a dusty, empty corner and got comfortable.

"You've lived in Lusty for how long, now?" Matthew asked quietly.

"Nearly six months. You should know that because you and Steven were busy putting the finishing touches on this place the day I came to town."

"Darlin', that was one of those rhetorical questions. I suppose you've never taken the opportunity to go and visit the Lusty Historical Society Museum, either."

Kelsey blinked and for extra measure gave her head a shake. She refocused on Matthew and ran his last statement through her brain. It was no good. He still wasn't making any sense. "No, I haven't. I don't see—"

"Come on." He took the flowers she'd been trying to hand back to him, then turned to her head waitress. "Hey, Michelle, will you put these in water for us? Thanks."

Michelle Parker, a Benedict cousin, nodded happily and came right over, relieving Matthew of the small bouquet.

"Ooh, they're so pretty. Yellow rosebuds and baby's breath. I'll see to them right away." Michelle beamed a smile at them both, then spun her heel and headed for the kitchen.

Matthew reached for Kelsey's hand and began to lead her toward the door.

"What...you can't just pull me out of my restaurant in the middle of the day. I have things to do here!"

Matthew stopped and shot her a smile that did unspeakably mushy things to her resolve. "You're between lunch and dinner. Can't you spare twenty minutes or so? It's important."

Well, when he put it like that, she supposed she could give him a bit of time. She did have everything under control in the kitchen. Tracy Jessop, her *sous-chef*, could take care of things for a while. In fact, Kelsey often used this time of day to run errands or take a nice long break. She guessed she could consider accompanying Matthew to be both.

Still, she made her response border on the edge of grudging. "All right. If it's important, I'll go with you."

"Thank you, sweetheart."

Kelsey tried not to think how the sound of that endearment warmed her belly or how good it felt having her hand in Matthew Benedict's as they set out to walk the few blocks to the Lusty Historical Society's building.

She'd noticed the museum, of course, and passed it every day on her way to work. In the six months she'd been living in the small town of Lusty, Texas, she'd never once visited the place.

"Hey, there."

Kelsey hadn't noticed the Jeep pull up to the curb just ahead of them, nor had she noticed the tall, broad shouldered, dark-haired man who stepped out of it until he greeted them.

"Hey, bro, good timing," Matthew said.

Steven Benedict was as handsome as his fair-haired brother and, for reasons Kelsey had never looked at seriously, just as appealing to her hormones. No one could be more surprised than she that those pesky female bits had begun to emerge from their five-year long slumber. She'd thought to never feel attraction to any man again, let alone experience it for two at the same time.

"Where are we off to?" Steven put himself on Kelsey's other side and took her left hand in his right.

Oh, my. She'd never before had both hands held by men who were too damn handsome for their own good. They had been dropping in for meals, or to flirt, or to give her gifts for the last couple of months.

She could admit to herself they were nice to look at and that she even enjoyed their company. She just wasn't planning to date, let alone get serious about anybody. Not ever again.

There was only so much heartbreak and loss a body could stand.

"We're off to the museum," Matthew said.

"'Bout time," Steven said. Then he turned and smiled at her. "How you doing today, sweetheart?"

"I was doing considerably better until Matthew said the two of you want to share me."

She didn't know what she expected Steven Benedict to say to that, but she was pretty certain she hadn't been expecting his eager nod of agreement.

"That's right," Steven said quietly. "It's the Benedict way. Why do you think this town was named Lusty?"

"I...I guess I've never really given it a lot of thought. I've heard of some interesting town names. I guess I just figured Lusty was one of them." Kelsey had the feeling that everyone knew something about her new home town she didn't. They passed several people on the street, and every one of them took note of the way the three of them were walking—hand in hand in hand—and smiled.

"There's a reason for this town's name," Steven said.

"It's an interesting story. That's for certain," Matthew said. "One that we're eager to share with you."

* * * *

Matthew wasn't ashamed to admit the museum was one of his favorite places in Lusty. To step through the doors of the small building was to step back in time.

He smiled as he always did at the photograph that greeted every visitor on their arrival. How fitting that this would be the first image everyone saw. In the photo, two women sat in chairs, each with two men behind her. Those men touched their woman with a proprietary grace Matthew appreciated.

Kelsey stepped forward and read the caption aloud. "Caleb, Joshua, and Sarah Benedict, with Adam Kendall, Warren Jessop, and Amanda Jessop-Kendall. July 4, 1883." She turned to Matthew.

"There are a lot of Benedicts and Kendalls and Jessops in town." She
shot a glance at Steven likely, Matthew thought, to be sure she
included him in the conversation. "Your ancestors?"

Matthew nodded. One quick glance at his brother and he knew
Steven believed what he did—that Kelsey *still* didn't understand.

"Caleb and Joshua were Sarah's husbands, just as Adam and
Warren were Amanda's."

"*Husbands*? Oh. You mean, she was married to one, and then got
married to the other?"

"No," Matthew said. "She belonged to them both at the same
time."

"The Benedict way," Steven confirmed. "It started with them.
Caleb and Joshua were twins—another family trait. Sarah fell in love
with them both and knew she couldn't choose between them, and that
was just fine with those brothers Benedict."

Kelsey looked from Matthew, to Steven, then put her gaze back
on the photograph.

"I thought…When I had dinner with your family, I thought how
civilized it was for your mom, dad, and step-dad to all live together."

Steven chuckled. "No, baby. Our mom lives with our dads.
Period."

"Susan said that just about everyone who lived in Lusty was
family of a sort." Kelsey's voice sounded distracted. She looked at the
photo again.

"Amanda was Sarah's cousin, came west from Richmond on a
quest. Once she got here, she met Adam and Warren, who already
were a couple," Matthew said. "They fell in love with her and had to
work to convince her to stay."

"The men were bisexual in the eighteen hundreds? That would
have been dangerous for them—for all of them!" Kelsey said.

"It was dangerous and illegal," Steven said. "It was actually the
Jessop-Kendalls who conceived of the idea of a town, an autonomous
place where they could live as they chose and in privacy with their

friends nearby. As you can imagine, our great-greats signed on to that. It never says in any of the journals why they named the town Lusty, though."

"Perhaps they thought the answer to that question obvious."

There were photos of the Big House, as the original Benedict homestead was called today, and of the "new house," the large mansion built close to it that was the original home of the Jessop-Kendalls.

Kelsey continued to peruse the items on display. As she did, a door in the back opened and a middle-aged woman came into the room.

"Hey, Aunt Anna," Matthew said in greeting.

"Why hello there, Matthew and Steven. You've brought your girl around, I see."

Kelsey' jaw dropped, and she looked as though she was in shock. Matthew made a mental note to speak to all his well-meaning relatives. He didn't want them scaring Kelsey off before they had her.

"Kelsey, you've met our aunt, Anna Jessop?" Steven stepped into the breach, and Matthew sighed in relief.

"I don't think we've been introduced," Kelsey said.

"You make very good food." Aunt Anna shook Kelsey's hand. "Just go on and look around. We're very proud of our history here in Lusty. And we have a fine collection of photographs and other relics. 'Course, there's more up at the Big House."

Matthew led Kelsey over to a series of photographs. "Once they'd formed the town, they invited select people to come and live with them. The first were Amanda's mother and a friend of Amanda's who also happened to be a lawyer and who knew Warren Jessop. His name was Terence Parks, and once Terence felt settled and secure, his friend and lover Jeremy Jones came and joined him. He was an artist, a photographer, and took all the photos on display here."

Matthew let her look, sending questioning glances to his brother behind her back when she leaned in to look at the inscription below one particular portrait.

"This card says that's Bat Masterson with the Benedicts."

"That's right," Steven said.

"*The* Bat Masterson?"

"Yeah, he was a friend of the family," Matthew said. And then, because he was so damn proud of his forebears, he pointed to another photo. "Another family friend," he said

"Wyatt Earp." Kelsey's tone reflected awe.

She continued to look at the photos, at other generations of their family. Matthew felt pride in his roots and knew Steven did, too. There was so much more he wanted to tell Kelsey but contented himself with simply following her as she stopped at each photograph and display case. She didn't rush but seemed to take everything in. The museum wasn't large by anyone's definition of the word. Soon they were back where they'd started, near the front door.

Kelsey turned and faced Matt and his brother.

"I think I'm beginning to understand. It's natural for you to think in terms of sharing a woman sexually. So you haven't been playing some kind of one-upmanship game with me at all. You've both been, to use your word, wooing me, because you want to have sex with me. Both of you. At the same time."

Matthew couldn't read Kelsey's mood or her state of mind. Her expression blank, she'd spoken almost clinically. He supposed he couldn't blame her for that, though he'd wanted to wince when she'd said "have sex" instead of "make love." If another woman had said that, it wouldn't have bothered him. But this was Kelsey, and while he knew that when he and Steven finally had her between them they'd be making love to her, he understood where her thoughts had led her.

So he nodded and said, "Yes. Steven and I both want to have sex with you at the same time."

Steven nodded, then slipped his hands into his jeans pockets, a sure sign he was nervous. Kelsey looked from one to the other of them for a long moment. Finally, she nodded, a curt little jerk of her head that told Matthew her decision had just made her very nervous.

"I need to think about this. Obviously, the two of you have been planning…considering…" Kelsey waved her hands in the air almost, Matthew thought, as if she was trying to grasp something to hang on to.

Matthew stilled her hands with both of his. "No, Kelsey. We've been hoping, mostly." He could have told her that in the last couple of months, as they'd talked from time to time, gotten to know her better, they both understood her resolve not to get involved romantically. She'd turned both him and Steven down when they'd each, in turn, asked her out on a date.

However, in the last few weeks especially, they'd each noticed a change in her reaction to them.

"I close up at ten tonight. You can pick me up then. We can go someplace and talk about this."

"We can go to the ranch." Steven exhaled and looked at Matt. "We'll take you to the ranch."

Before either he or his brother could say another word, Kelsey stepped around them and exited the museum.

Matthew looked at Steven. His brother's brow furrowed, and he rocked back on his heels.

"Holy hell," Steven said, his tone just above a whisper. "She still doesn't get it."

"It took her a few months of living here before she ever became aware of either one of us as *men*." Matthew continued to look at the door where Kelsey had just exited. "After what she's been through, I suppose it shouldn't surprise either one of us she would think we only want sex."

"You're right. We knew this wasn't going to be easy, but that's okay. She's the woman we love, so we'll do what it takes. So now what do we do?" Steven asked.

Matthew grinned. "She's so responsive to us both. We've both seen it in her eyes when we've talked with her. We'll know when we see her tonight if she's leaning toward us. If she is then there's really only one thing we can do. We seduce her into our bed. Then we fuck her brains out and get her body so addicted to ours that her heart has no choice but to join in."

"Okay, that sounds like a pretty good plan."

Matthew thought it did, too. He just hoped to hell it worked.

Chapter 2

Oh my God, I can't believe I just did that.

Kelsey kept her pace brisk as she covered the distance between the Lusty Historical Society Museum and her restaurant. She didn't think the men would follow her, not now when she'd agreed to think about what they apparently wanted.

She put on her business smile as she entered her domain, nodded to the patrons who looked up and gave her a wave or a howdy, but kept her demeanor all business. She didn't want to talk to anyone right now. A fine tremor worked its way up from her belly, spreading out to her limbs. She headed straight to her small office, closed and locked the door behind her, then slid, nearly boneless, into her chair.

"Oh, damn. Oh, damn." Her face flamed, and she covered it with both hands. Nothing to do but to wait out the shakes and the blush. Inhaling deeply, Kelsey closed her eyes, leaned back in her chair, and focused on relaxing her jittery body.

Not a panic attack. No, what she felt at the moment wasn't one of those. Relief washed through her. She'd not had a panic attack in the last year but had experienced them often enough just after the shooting that she'd come to dread them.

Her eyes opened, and she her gaze roam around her small office. This was her dream come true, a restaurant of her own, and while she didn't own the building, she owned the business, and the menu, and the *essence* of it.

Business had been brisk since opening day. While Kelsey had braced herself for the possibility of failure, three out of five new businesses did that in the first two years, in her heart she knew her business would continue to grow and prosper.

Her eyes landed on the framed newspaper article on her wall. When the food editor of the Waco *Tribune-Herald* had contacted her last month, of course she'd said yes to the interview and the feature. What restaurateur wouldn't? It had never occurred to her the reporter would mention her personal tragedy of years before. She'd cringed, reading that part of it. So far, though, the responses she'd gotten from that article had been positive. Lusty Appetites had experienced an influx of business from the larger city. People, it seemed, didn't mind driving more than an hour to enjoy her food. She knew they did enjoy it because she'd developed a clientele from Waco and surrounding area. Her business was growing? Hell, at the moment, it was thriving.

Just as she, personally, had begun to thrive. She'd stopped believing herself capable of personal happiness in the aftermath of the shooting. In those dark first days after watching the horror unfold before her, she'd been tempted to end her own life.

Only the sure and certain knowledge that act would have disappointed Philip and dishonored Sean held her back. So she'd put away those thoughts and chosen life.

Not the full blown, all-out, grab-all-the-joy-you-can kind of life some seemed destined for and able to achieve so easily. No, her life would be measured and neat, she would set goals, achieve them, and then do what she could to give back.

So why the hell had she just told two handsome, buff men that she would seriously consider having sex with them both at the same time?

"Oh, my God." Kelsey was still shaking. She held up her hands to watch them tremble as the unwelcome truth settled in her thoughts. She shook, not with embarrassment or dread, but with *excitement*.

More than five years had passed since she'd had sex, and while the grief counselor had told her she would eventually heal to the point where she'd seek intimacy again, Kelsey hadn't believed her.

Having sex with two men at the same time was not life as Kelsey Madison had mapped it out when she'd decided to move to Lusty, Texas.

Still, she couldn't deny the flutters in her belly or that for some time now just thinking about the brothers Benedict made her nipples tight and her pussy wet.

All right, time to regroup. She knew if she wanted to, she could call Matthew or Steven and tell them no. She didn't have to go through with meeting with them this evening just because she'd said she would. She had choices and options. No was always an option.

Obviously her body needed some attention of the sexual variety. Her female parts, overflowing with estrogen and with no place to put it, had begun demanding action.

Kelsey let her thoughts wander back to the museum.

What the hell would you call that, anyway? Serial menagerie?

Her giggles erupted as the reality that she'd pretty much decided to have sex with two men at the same time hit her.

She was a healthy woman with a healthy libido and what she'd always considered an average imagination. There'd been a time or two, before meeting Philip, when she'd brought herself to orgasm thanks to the fantasy of having two cocks all to herself.

Now here was the opportunity to bring those long ago, lusty fantasies to life.

Oh, yeah, I get the town's name now.

Kelsey's mind circled back to the loss of her family and those long ago promises to herself. Recalling, too, the predictions of her therapist, she tried to set aside her arousal and think.

There was intimacy, and then there was *intimacy*.

Cut to the chase, Kels.

Kelsey had always been honest with herself. She wasn't about to change that trait now. She could have sex with those two rocking studs. It didn't mean she was going to fall in love with them or that she would marry either of them.

So why not just go ahead and have sex? They were all three of them unattached adults.

Despite the reactions of her body, she knew falling in love with anyone ever again was simply out of the question.

Her heart had shattered as she'd watched a crazed killer gun down her husband and young son five years before.

There simply was nothing left of that part of her to give to anyone anymore.

* * * *

Steven turned to look at his brother. A smile tugged at the corner of his mouth when he read the expression of satisfaction on Matthew's face. He hated to play Mr. Obvious, but that was a part of his nature.

"Just because she said we could pick her up doesn't mean she'll come to bed with us."

Matthew shook his head, but his smile didn't diminish. "Yeah, I know. And even if she does come with us, and *come* with us, it doesn't mean the campaign to win her heart is over."

Steven looked over at his Aunt Anna, who seemed to be reading a magazine as she stood by the information counter. He knew his aunt very well, however. "Let's go," he said to his brother.

Matt got it. They each waved good-bye to their aunt and stepped out into the afternoon sun.

"No," he said to Matthew as they headed toward his Jeep, "I don't imagine winning Kelsey's heart is going to be easy."

"I simply can't imagine," Matthew said. "I know what a blow it was for me when I walked in and found Linda in bed with another man." Matthew pulled his sunglasses out of the V opening of his shirt and jammed them onto his face.

Steven knew the shades weren't only because of the bright sunlight.

"That leveled me, and I didn't want to get involved with anyone for a long time. I can't imagine what it would have been like to see a wife and child shot to death in front of me," Matthew said.

"No, neither of us can really understand the magnitude of that kind of loss."

Matthew rested against the fender of Steven's Jeep. Steven copied his position so they stood side by side. He nodded, as his brother did, to some of the passersby. One of the things Steven loved best about this small town showed itself now. People could see they were having a serious discussion and left them to it.

"I think it's a good sign that she's begun to notice us," Matthew said. "That's why I thought we had to begin our campaign right away. I didn't want to take the chance that our beautiful butterfly would emerge from her cocoon and fall for someone else."

Steven agreed completely with Matt's assessment. "I also noticed her agreement to think about our offer lacked warmth. What do you want to bet the lady figures she can have sex with us to scratch her various itches, but that's it?"

"Not taking that bet because that's what I think, too. That means there's only one thing for us to do. You realize that, don't you?"

"Oh, yeah." Steven smiled. When it came to the important things in life, he and his brother had always been on the same page. He loved all his siblings, but it had always been Matthew, older than him by a year, with whom he'd shared the closest connection. He'd never doubted, even in those dark days after his brother had married Linda, that they would also one day share a wife.

Now, he turned and gave his big brother a wide smile. "You know what else I think? I think we need to give the lady so much love and affection and attention that she becomes addicted to us before she even sees it happening."

Matthew straightened from the Jeep and clapped him on the shoulder. "That won't be a hardship, brother. Well, I have another couple of hours to put in at the office."

"I'm heading home to get things ready for tonight."

They agreed that Matthew should drive out to the ranch—a 1950s home the family had built a couple of miles outside of town—and then ride back into town with Steven to pick up Kelsey.

Steven got into the Jeep and sat just a moment more. His thoughts were on Kelsey and the evening ahead. She'd said she was just going to think about letting him and his brother both love her. Even though she hadn't said yes, Steven wanted to be prepared. That meant condoms. Steven didn't need any more time to know that Kelsey was the woman he wanted to spend the rest of his life with. A part of him wanted desperately to fill the hole in her mother's heart with their child, either his or Matthew's. It made no difference, but it was way too soon for that.

As he started the vehicle and pulled into traffic, he decided he'd better see what he could do about protection. Of course, he'd buy those condoms elsewhere. No need feeding the Lusty gossips any fresh fodder.

* * * *

"We like the look of you, Connors. Your résumé is downright impressive."

Wesley Connors flushed, the praise coming from someone as influential in the state-wide political scene as Sherman Fremont nearly enough to make his head spin. The exclusive Faraday Club in Austin boasted a membership list of not only frontline celebrities, but the movers and shakers of government, too.

Connors soaked up the rarified atmosphere like a parched man slurping water from a fountain. He'd worked long and hard over the last four years to contribute to the party and make a difference. He'd put in hundreds of hours as a volunteer with three separate charities, he'd married "up," and he'd been nominated as business innovator of the year.

Now all his hard work looked as though it was finally going to pay off.

"I don't usually make promises, but I'm going to make an exception in your case." Fremont leaned forward as though about to impart a secret. "You win the mayoral race with a margin of five percent or better, and you'll have my personal backing for state senator in two years."

State senator! That was several steps forward in his plan at one go. Mindful of his image, Connors lowered his eyes, giving the appearance of humility.

"Mr. Fremont, I simply don't know what to say. I had hoped to one day put my hat into the ring for the State House. But in two years? I'm honored, completely honored by your generosity and your confidence in me."

"Of course." Fremont signaled to the waiter who promptly brought the man another bottle of beer.

"Sir?" The waiter stood ready to get Connors whatever he wanted. Again, mindful of his image, he said, "Just water, please."

Fremont grunted, which Connors interpreted as approval. He waited until the waiter had returned with Connor's glass of ice water.

"Now, we're expecting you to slaughter your opponent, Connors. At the same time, we want to see a full-out media blitz. You take your campaign for mayor to the whole of Texas. Name recognition is the name of the game. I expect that by the time you're sworn in as Mayor, most of Texas will know your name."

"Statewide, sir?" Connors tried not to let his shock show. Fortunately, though he failed in that regard, Fremont assumed the reaction had a different cause.

"Yes, it's expensive. Don't worry about that. I'm making arrangements. You'll have the money you need to pull this off."

"Thank you, sir. I'm very grateful."

"Damn right you are," Fremont said. "You just remember that gratitude, and we're going to get along fine. Real fine."

Connors managed to maintain his composure throughout the rest of the meal. He didn't, in fact, allow himself to get nervous until he pulled into his driveway and watched the garage door open. Cora Lynn, his wife, was not yet home, which was a good thing. It would give him a bit of time to assimilate the good news–bad news revelations of this afternoon and settle his thoughts.

As he let himself into the house and headed for his office, he knew one thing for certain. Something had to be done.

He sat behind his desk and opened the locked drawer on the right. Reaching inside, he pulled out two pages he'd printed from the Internet.

One was a story from five years before, a brash and brazen holdup gone wrong that had shocked and saddened the entire city of Austin. A husband and father along with his young son had been shot to death in a convenience store robbery. Although the shooter had initially gotten away with the help of an accomplice driving a black sedan, he'd later been identified after the local news stations broadcasted the store's security video.

That shooter, hopped up on drugs, had died in a shootout with police. His accomplice, the man who'd driven the getaway car, had never been identified.

The story went on to detail how the crime was even that much more tragic, for the wife and mother of the victims had sat outside the store in the family car. It was believed she witnessed the shooting and the flight of the gunman.

Wesley set that article aside and picked up the other. This appeared a much happier piece about a restaurant in a small Texas town that was fast making a name for itself as the place to dine in the area. He'd come upon the article by chance when he'd been searching for information on the convenience store shootings. The article had referenced the crime, for the efficient reporter had made the connection—victim turned entrepreneur.

Just when Wesley believed he'd atoned for his sins, just when he was about to take the next step into a career that he hoped to bring him to the governor's office in Texas and maybe, just maybe as one recent Texas governor had done, to the nation's capital itself.

He looked down at the face of a pretty brunette. Her hair had been pulled back and out of the way. She used to wear it in a chic cut, just long enough to brush the bottom of her face. In this photograph, taken to accompany the article about her business, her mouth tilted up in a small smile.

The last time he'd seen her face she'd worn an expression of shock and horror, her wide eyes drilling his from behind the windshield of her car.

Wesley felt the meal he'd just eaten sour in his stomach. Sherman Fremont wanted a statewide media blitz, which would undoubtedly feature Connor's smiling face being flashed on the television screens and newspapers from Austin all the way to a small town he'd never heard of before.

He held up the page he'd printed and looked at the woman for a long time. He couldn't take the chance she'd see his face and remember him.

If he wanted the life he'd earned, the life he deserved, then he would have to do something about Kelsey Madison, and he'd have to do it soon.

Chapter 3

Kelsey placed her hand on her belly, a simple reaction to the butterflies that wouldn't settle there. Her last employee had just left. As she did every evening, she walked through the restaurant, seeing that everything had been turned off, closed up, and done.

At five minutes after ten, she stepped out onto the sidewalk and locked the door behind her.

They stood waiting for her, two handsome devils, one light, one dark, wearing identical expressions of mischief, mayhem, and mirth.

No, that last part was only her imagination. The brothers Benedict greeted her with smiles that truly warmed her, body and soul.

Enough of that, Kels. This is supposed to be about sex and nothing more.

Not surprisingly, she felt that reaction, too. Liquid warmth sped her heart and moistened her pussy. She'd focus on the physical and keep her soul out of it.

"Hey, pretty lady." Matthew held out his hand, and in that moment, she set aside her musings and simply went to them.

She felt her heart bump when Matthew took her hand and used it to pull her inexorably into his arms. His movements slow, as if not to frighten her, he wrapped his arms around her and laid his lips on hers.

Oh, God. She'd forgotten this, the sudden free fall into desire that the simple action of mouth on mouth could create. Soft and sultry, wet and wonderful, Matthew's tongue stroked her bottom lip, then swept into the cavern of her mouth, tasting her, learning her.

She tasted him in turn, his flavor the ambrosia she'd longed for. Their kiss became a sexy dance of tongues and lips, a slide and glide that turned her nipples into hard points of desire.

He lifted his mouth from hers, his eyes hooded, his smile more disarming that she'd ever seen it. She felt that smile sliding into her, under her skin, and felt powerless to stop it.

Before she could think of something clever to say to pull her back from the vortex, he gently brought her arms from around his neck and edged her just subtly to the left and into the arms of his brother.

Steven's mouth devoured hers, his arms hard and secure around her, pressing her to him chest-to-chest and thigh-to-thigh. He tasted different that Matthew, with more raw power and urgent need, and she felt helpless to do anything but surrender to his possession. A sense of safety stole over her, numbing her thoughts so she could only let herself go, let herself enjoy.

Carnal and captivating, his kiss fed the flames of her passion. The ridge pressing against her belly seemed to call to her, and her hips answered with a rolling, urgent thrust.

"I knew it." Steven's deep rumble vibrated inside her belly, and those butterflies took to performing aerial maneuvers. "I knew you'd taste like heaven."

Kelsey blinked, trying to regain her senses, struggling to get her mind working again.

She must have looked worried because Matthew chose that moment to step closer to her. Between them, they bracketed her, cocooned her in male heat and pheromones.

"It's all right, baby. No one drove past. The town's asleep."

"Good." She hadn't even *thought* about what anyone would think seeing her kiss one and then the other of the town's two most eligible bachelors.

"Come on, sweet thing. Let's take this party someplace more private." Steven placed another, this time chaste, kiss on her lips, rubbed a possessive hand down her back, and then stepped away.

Steven walked around to the driver's side while Matthew opened the passenger door and urged her into the front seat of the Jeep.

He got in after her, lifted her onto his lap, then wrapped the seat belt around them both.

"Are you sure this is legal?" she asked.

Matthew chuckled. "If the deputy sheriff doesn't complain, I wouldn't worry about it."

"*You're* the deputy sheriff." Kelsey practically melted against the hard male body under her. The press of his erection beneath her bottom made her juices flow even faster.

My God if I'm not careful I'm going to leak all over him.

Just then, Matthew pushed his hips up slightly, and Kelsey thought it a miracle she didn't come right then and there.

She needed to distract herself, fast. Using every bit of willpower she could muster, she searched for something safe to talk about. Her thoughts jumped ahead to their destination. Kelsey had never been to the Benedict ranch itself. She understood the operation and scale of the land was massive, even by Texas standards. "The Big House in town here was the original ranch house, wasn't it?"

"Yes, until the 1950s when Sarah Benedict and Amanda Jessop-Kendall, along with our grandparents, decided to cede more land to the town. It suited Sarah to live out the rest of her years in the house she'd moved into with her husbands, and it suited our grandparents, who were true ranchers, to build a new house away from the settled area, closer to the land they loved."

"Your grandmother knew Sarah?" There had been quite a bit in the museum about Sarah Carmichael Benedict. She'd been so beautiful, and Caleb and Joshua had seemed so handsome, it was no wonder they'd been attracted to each other.

"She knew Sarah *and* Amanda," Matthew said. "The men had already passed on when Grandma Kate met her husbands. She has some very interesting stories to tell about our great-greats."

"I met her one of the times I had dinner with your folks," Kelsey said. "One time, I think Susan said she was in Las Vegas."

"Grandma Kate loves to tour with a seniors group out of Waco. You never know where she'll take off to next," Steven said.

Both men's tones had softened when they'd spoken of their grandmother. Texan men loved their mothers and grandmothers, probably more, Kelsey thought, than the average American male. She couldn't recall too many male friends in Pennsylvania who'd displayed such sentimentality toward their older female relatives.

It didn't take long to leave the few lights of Lusty behind. Minutes later, Steven slowed the Jeep and turned onto a lane.

No clouds marred the sky, allowing the full moon to bathe the landscape in a silvery luminescence. The lane proved long and gently curving. They drove up a slight rise.

When they crested the small hill, Sarah gasped. Before her, nestled in a small dale, stood an enormous home, two-story and sprawling, white with a wrap-around porch. Behind the house and to the left, she could see a barn. Corrals formed a patchwork pattern around that building. Even in the moonlight she could see horses grazing.

"It's beautiful. And so big!"

"We tend to have large families," Steven said. "My grandparents had five children, which made for eight people living in the house at one time. Plus, there had to be a couple of guest rooms ready for whatever family wanted to visit."

"And now you live here alone?" Kelsey couldn't imagine having such a large, magnificent house to herself. Here was a reminder of one very important fact about the brothers Benedict, something she tended to forget. The family was as rich as Midas.

"It's just a house, sweetheart," Matthew said. His words, accompanied by a slight hug, told her he could read her moods, could almost read her thoughts. That couldn't be good for her continued emotional equilibrium.

"Sometimes, I have so many family members staying over, I wish I *did* have the place to myself," Steven said. His light tone pushed back the uneasiness that had begun to creep up on her.

A porch light burned, a single silent greeting that took the edge of furtiveness away and made the mansion seem more home-like. It left her feeling—well, if not relaxed—at least a little less tense.

"Come on." Steven had gotten out and come around to the passenger side of the Jeep. Kelsey blinked because she'd been so tied up in her thoughts she'd not even noticed him moving.

Matthew unbuckled the seatbelt, and Steven easily lifted her out of the vehicle and into his arms.

"You're both so very strong." She knew it an inane thing to say, but she felt so surrounded by their strength, their maleness, that her usual defenses had been short-circuited.

He set her on her feet but held her close. "We would never hurt you, not either of us, sweetheart." Steven's softly spoken assurance came swiftly, and Kelsey worried that she might have hurt his feelings.

"I know you won't." She wouldn't have come with them if she'd had any doubts about her personal safety.

Matthew placed his hand on her back, stroking it up and down, the action both soothing and arousing.

"I liked the taste of you, Kelsey, and the way you melted in my arms. Are you going to let us have you?"

She could have protested that just because she'd kissed them didn't mean she was going to let them into her body. She could have but didn't. She was no hypocrite. If she was to be perfectly honest with herself, she had to admit the truth. She wanted these two men and the temptation they offered. A part of her had hoped they would simply sweep her up to their bedroom, but she would own her decisions and her actions.

"Yes. Yes, I want you both."

"Then come inside with us, sweetheart," Matthew said.

The interior of the house spoke of a life lived in quiet elegance. The entry hall featured a large chandelier, a sparkling fixture that softly illuminated the round room, devoid of furnishings save a polished wooden table, a mirror on the wall above it, and a coat tree. Marble underfoot, rich oak framing the doorways, the room smelled and felt like exactly what it was, the entrance into a world far different from the one Kelsey was used to.

"I've some champagne chilling," Steven said. "This way."

As they had just that afternoon, the brothers each took one of her hands. Their heat sank into her and the scent of them surrounded her, and in the space of time it took them to ascend the stairs to the second level, her thoughts quieted and her hormones began to riot.

They led her down a corridor toward the back of the house. Steven opened the last door on the right and stepped aside, allowing her to enter first.

She didn't know what impressed her more, the luxurious space, the wide open balcony doors, or the bed.

"That is the largest bed I have ever seen in my life." She'd not meant to say that aloud, but the sheer size of the thing robbed her of decorum.

"Another family tradition." Matthew stepped up behind her and placed his hands on her shoulders, his touch both warming and grounding her. How had he known the immensity of the bed would unnerve her?

"Whose bedroom is this?" A silly question, she'd bet, since it clearly had to be the largest in the house. The furnishings seemed decidedly feminine, though. Actually, the dusty rose carpet, grey walls, and white, gold and turquoise accents appealed to her completely. The dresser appeared to be cherry wood, her very favorite.

"This is the master bedroom," Steven said.

"Yours, then." Of course, it had to be.

"Not yet."

Before she could think about that cryptic response, he went over to a dresser and the CD player that sat there. Soft music filled the room. Next, he picked up a long match, struck it, and began lighting candles.

She hadn't noticed them scattered around the room. He'd given thought to where to put them, obviously keeping them out of the fresh breeze that wafted gently through the window.

The setting made her uncomfortable. "I don't need romance." She didn't for one moment want to think about romance. This was sex, pure and simple.

Focus on the physical.

"Not romance, Kelsey," Matthew whispered in her ear. "Seduction."

His words brushed against the shell of her ear, sending a shiver skittering down her spine. A sound of male interest drew her attention to the man slowly walking toward her. Everything about him turned her on, from his sexy saunter to the way he blew out the long match and set it on the dresser. Wrapped in Matthew's warmth while seeing the lust in Steven's eyes reminded her that a sexual fantasy was about to come to vivid, heart-pounding, orgasmic life.

"You nipples just peaked, hard little points of lust just waiting for our hands and our mouths," Steven said.

How could words turn her knees weak? Before she could respond, he stepped up to her and cupped her face in his hands. "Hello, sweet Kelsey." And he sealed his greeting against her lips.

You don't need candles and music to seduce me.

The thought flitted away, leaving her head empty and her body suddenly ravenous. The touch of his mouth, the sweep of his tongue, and gently possessive cupping of his hands seduced her completely. Never had a kiss tasted of raw sex, and never had she felt herself grow so wet so fast.

Matthew pressed closer to her back as Steven continued to woo her lips with his. The flavor of him, exotic, erotic, addicted her on the spot, consumed her in a way she'd never known existed.

Soft lips teased along the back of her neck as hands, finely trembling, brushed across her back and then down, to stroke the globes of her ass. They slid around the front of her, palms pressing flat against her pussy, the heat searing and incredible.

Steven stepped back, licking his lips as if to hold on to the taste of her. Matthew tugged gently on her hair and she tilted her neck back and surrendered her mouth to him.

Slow, lazy, his tongue wooed hers, his possession just as deep, just as arousing as his brother's had been.

Steven stepped forward and softly caressed her breasts. A light tug, and the buttons of her simple cotton blouse fell open, one by one.

"Mmm." Hot breath formed the sound against her chest, and the moist tribute hardened her already pointed nipples nearly to the point of pain.

Matthew's lips continued to suck on hers as if he could, by this single act, devour her. Steven slid her blouse off her shoulders, and his fingers slipped free the button on her skirt, slid the zipper down, and gently nudged the fabric past her feminine hips.

"Step out, sweetheart."

Kelsey didn't want to relinquish Matthew's kiss just yet, so she gave herself over to Steven as he lifted one foot and then the other until her skirt no longer covered her feet.

The brush of a hand over her lace-covered curls made her shudder. Matthew drew back and traced her moist lip with the pad of his thumb.

"You taste ripe and lush, Kelsey. And you're so damn responsive."

She didn't care if her tremors gave her away. She didn't care if these men knew how desperately she hungered for the touch, the feel of male possession. Sex at its best should be raw and hungry.

"I need more. I need it all."

"Oh, you're going to get it all. You're going to get all of us." Matthew reached behind her with one hand and slipped open the hooks of her bra.

She felt the lace give way. As Matthew drew it from her body, Steven got down on his knees in front of her and eased her panties down.

She felt a puff of warm, moist breath and then he set his mouth on her.

Chapter 4

Matthew caught her as her knees buckled.

His chuckle, smug male, only added to the heat building inside her. On his knees in front of her, Steven nudged her legs apart with his shoulders, his hands cupping her bottom as he feasted on her cunt.

Hot, wet, his tongue spread shivery delight all through her. He drank her essence, the flow of moisture she couldn't help, and he sucked every bit of strength and willpower from her body.

Humming, he continued to use lips and tongue and teeth to pleasure her. The vibration of that sound excited her completely, an electric shock to a body too long devoid of arousal.

Kelsey came, a tsunami of lush rapture drowning her, pulling her down deeper and deeper into the world of Eros so that nothing else existed but the fiery fingers of climactic pleasure consuming her.

"Damn, woman," Steven said.

She could barely keep track of the moment. Even as Matthew lifted her and laid her on the bed, she was aware of Steven tearing the clothes from his body, reaching for her. Matthew handed him something, and she heard the tear of foil, but the act of protection didn't slow him down one bit.

Then he was between her thighs, his large body, gloriously naked, coming down on her. The orgasm had ebbed, but the brief sight of his cock as well as the look of hunger on his face immediately sparked her ardor.

The heat of Steven's body covered her at the same time his cock pressed between the folds of her pussy. He entered her in one powerful thrust.

"Oh, God." The fullness, the stretching fed a hunger she'd suppressed. The weight of a lover pressing over her, into her, fed a need she'd forgotten.

"You're so hot and tight, baby," Steven said. "*So good.*"

The words brushed her face, and she had the sudden sense that he wanted to kiss her but held back. Determined to take and give in equal measure, Kelsey bowed up, fastened her mouth on his and tasted her own juices on his lips.

He surged into her, his cock seeming to grow even larger as he wrapped his arms around her and plundered her, above and below. His tongue dipped, delved, dominated as his cock thrust inside her, hard and fast and deep.

Kelsey wrapped her arms and legs around him, holding tight as her second climax sizzled her synapses and shivered her senses. She cried out, a feral screech of ecstasy erupting from deep inside her.

"Yes." Steven thrust hard and held himself deep, and even as Kelsey continued to come, she felt his cock inside her pulse his own climax.

Kelsey let her arms fall to the bed. Eyes closed, she swore she could see stars. As she struggled for breath, sound and sense began to penetrate her fogged brain. Music played, and the scent of candles, lavender and citrus, mixed with the scent of sex, the aroma at once restful and arousing. Weight and heat separated from her body as Steven edged himself off. His breathing sounded as labored as hers, and she wondered if he felt as wrecked as she. Two orgasms. She'd never in her life had two orgasms in the space of a few minutes.

Before that thought could fully sink in, the bed dipped, and a hot, hard, naked male body pressed against her right side.

"Do you have any idea how beautiful you are when you come?" Matthew's whispered words kissed against her neck. When he used his hand to turn her head toward him, she opened her eyes and her lips.

The press of his erect penis against her stirred her fires, adding fuel so that they began to burn anew. She turned on her side, threw her left leg over his hip and reached for his cock.

Hot and hard, his latex covered organ defied her hand's ability to fist it completely. Her fingers barely touched, and as she pumped him, as her mouth took his, he surged into her hand and grew.

She plunged her tongue into his mouth and gave herself permission to pillage.

Hot and wild and free, she moved up, moved over, and took. Her mouth, eager for every flavor of this man, nibbled and tasted, learned and explored. She couldn't marshal this need inside her to take and take and *take*. It burned deep, demanding, this new instinct driving her to reckless abandon as she'd never been driven before.

She would have taken more, she would have taken all of him, but he rose up, strong, dominant, and fairly tossed her onto her stomach on the bed.

Matthew growled as he covered her He used his knees to nudge her onto her own. He nipped her shoulder with his teeth as he thrust into her from behind.

"Yeah. Oh, God, Kelsey, you feel so fucking good." He began to thrust in her, his control of her absolute. One hand found and squeezed her breast as the other wrapped around her middle. Palm open on her abdomen, his fingers spread wide, and she wondered if he could feel his own cock with his palm because it seemed to drive so deep into her.

His thrusts became sharper, faster, and Kelsey tilted her hips, raising her ass and splaying her legs to give him all she could. The need inside her spiraled out of control, became a raging scream for fulfillment such as she'd never known. Hornier, higher than she'd ever been, her orgasm eluded her, dared her to take more, and then still more.

"Oh, God, Matthew. *Please!*" Her thoughts scattered, literally floating out of her. There was no room for thinking, only for feeling, only for the physical.

Matthew heard her and understood her. She hadn't expected or wanted this connection, but that didn't matter. The connection between her and this man and his brother had been forged, grew strong, and fed on every part of her.

"Yes, Kelsey, take it. Take it, baby."

His voice crooned as his hand slid down lower to allow his fingers to find her clit. Kelsey screamed as she came, the orgasm exploding out of her, every part of her shaking, feeling, coming, until her body collapsed, her face on the pillow, the climax throbbing through her making her cunt grip and spasm around the cock inside her. She felt his ejaculation and wondered, vaguely, if she would ever be the same again.

Matthew collapsed on top of her, his body heavy but warm and so good she closed her eyes in pleasure. Tiny aftershocks washed through her, and her nipples pinched so tight they hurt.

Matthew lifted himself off her, and the breeze from the window chilled her sweat-dampened body. She shivered, but only once, because a sheet covered her, and then she was joined under it by both men, one on either side.

Steven stroked a hand down her hair. "You've needed this for a long time, sweetheart," he said.

Kelsey could only manage a grunt in response.

"Now that we've taken the edge off for you, we'll have some champagne and a soak in the hot tub. Then we can love you properly."

More? Kelsey honestly didn't know if her body could take more. She managed to turn over. Flopping onto her back, she blinked until two handsome, dampened-by-exertion faces smiled down at her. Her mind seized only one sentence, the one that seemed the most outrageous.

"Taken the edge off for me?"

"Well, sure," Steven said. "We knew it had been a long time for you, and we knew how hot you were burning for us. So we figured a couple of quickies should level the playing field, so to speak."

Kelsey didn't know whether she wanted to laugh or hit him. She guessed he read her expression because he bent over her and placed a quick kiss on her lips. She saw the laughter in his eyes, but before she could raise the energy to hit him, Matthew stroked his hand down her body.

"Besides, we promised to have you at the same time, and we've not done that yet. We don't want you to think we're not men of our word."

Kelsey felt her mouth open in a complete O of surprise. "We didn't just—"

"Oh, no, babe, that was definitely two instances of one on one. We're going after two on one, or should I say, two *in* one. Us being the two, and you being the one," Steven said.

"But..."

"While we're soaking, you can tell us how you want us," Matthew said.

Kelsey wasn't given any more time to think on the matter. Matthew pulled the sheet off her, and Steven scooped her into his arms.

She started to struggle when she realized she was being carried, completely naked, out to the balcony.

"We're private here, baby." Steven subdued her easily. Overhead, the moon shone down, and the summer air kissed her flesh, drying the rest of her sweat and teasing her nostrils with the scent of honeysuckle.

The balcony was massive, and in the corner, bubbling away, a hot tub beckoned. Beside the tub stood an ice bucket, bottle of champagne at the ready.

Steven got into the tub with her, cradling her as the hot water enveloped her. Her sigh as the water soothed her elicited chuckles from both men.

It occurred to her she didn't mind their laughing at her, that she felt completely at ease and relaxed. She might worry about that later, but right now, she simply didn't care.

* * * *

"Here." Matthew handed Kelsey a glass of champagne, then gave one to Steven. He picked up his own glass and wondered if the combination of heat and alcohol would be too much for their woman.

Their woman.

God, he loved the sound of that, the way that thought fit so easily in his mind. He'd taken her harder than he'd meant to, but she'd more than matched him in strength and passion.

She matched him completely.

He looked up, his gaze meeting that of his brother's. He and Steven had always been close, closer to each other than any of their other siblings. A part of him had always known that one day he and Steven would fall in love with the same woman.

He'd rebelled when he'd been an asshole of twenty-one, had left home and gone to Chicago, determined to live his own life, make his own choices, hoe his own row.

He'd made a complete and utter mess of things.

"Oh, God," Kelsey sighed, closed her eyes, and eased herself back in the water.

"Want me to take your glass, sweetheart?" he asked.

"No. I want more." She opened her eyes, met his gaze, then looked at Steven. "I want more," she repeated.

More champagne, more of them.

"We want more, too," Steven said, and he stroked his hand down Kelsey's arm.

When his brother looked at him, Matthew nodded. "Not just more tonight," Matthew said. "More, period. This isn't a one night stand."

Matthew read the emotions that flitted, ever so briefly, across Kelsey's face. Before she could argue—and he knew she would, eventually—he bent down and kissed her lightly.

"We clicked," he explained. "Sexual partners don't always. No reason not to take time and explore all our appetites, is there?"

It proved harder than he believed it would, keeping that nonchalant expression on his face, acting as though what he and Steven already shared with her was nothing more than sex.

He was already falling in love with her, and he knew Steven felt the same.

"No," she replied at last, her expression telling him she felt relief at the way he'd posed the question. "No reason not to grab all we can before it burns out."

He wanted to but didn't ask her what would happen if it didn't burn out. The expression in his brother's eyes told him Steven fought the same battle. Matthew took comfort in the fact that Kelsey couldn't see it, couldn't read the love Steven held for her in his eyes, and knew it was because she wasn't looking for it. If she couldn't see it, it couldn't frighten her away.

A fine kind of tension had come over her, and he knew that sharp mind of hers would wake up at any moment and begin to think things through.

That was not in his, or Steven's, game plan.

He leaned closer to her and used his tongue to moisten her ear. When she shivered, he eased the glass from her fingers.

"Have you ever taken a cock in your ass?"

Kelsey inhaled sharply. Matthew darted his gaze down, saw her nipples had puckered anew, and smiled.

"Once. A long time ago. I don't think I cared for the experience."

"There are a couple of ways we can take you at the same time. Three, actually, that I can think of. One, we can stretch your pussy so that you'll have both our cocks in your cunt at the same time. I know it's possible, as I've been a bad boy and watched a few…um…interesting movies."

Kelsey giggled, a sound Matthew had never thought to hear from his too-serious love.

"Two," he continued on, not giving her a moment to answer, "you can suck one of us off while the other fucks your cunt." He used his tongue on the shell of her ear again, taking advantage of the hot response she had to that action. "And three," he used a finger to turn her face toward his. "Three is you take one of us in your ass and the other in your cunt. You get any two of the above three. Oh, time's up. Number one gets thrown out of the mix. Guess you're stuck with numbers two and three."

Kelsey tilted her head to the side, and he knew she would try to make light of his heavy-handedness. He could tell her that wouldn't make a difference. He'd seen the passion flare in her eyes.

"Do you really think you can talk me into taking your cock in my ass?"

Oh, he loved the way she asked that, one eyebrow raised, as if she knew he couldn't. He'd already known loving Kelsey was going to be hot and wild. Now he knew it was going to be fun, too.

"Talk you into it? Darling, before we're done with you, you're going to *beg* us for it."

Chapter 5

Kelsey knew she should laugh at that outrageous claim. The only problem was, she had the distinct feeling Matthew Benedict had just spoken nothing but the truth.

She didn't let her thoughts go back to that one time she'd tried anal sex. At first it had felt pretty damn good, but then—no. No thinking back over the past. Until this night, she'd had only two lovers in her life.

Keep the past in the past.

This was here and now, and only the moment mattered. She no longer looked for anything more than that.

In this moment she sat naked in a hot tub with two of the most virile, sexy men she'd ever known. She cast her glance down at Matthew, then aside to Steven.

They were both hard. If she'd ever considered the matter, she would have sworn that having three orgasms in one night would be an impossibility for her.

Looks like I'm about to set a new personal best.

She didn't want to think about how turned on she got when both men had gone all macho on her earlier. She'd decided to begin this ménage relationship with both eyes wide open—so to speak. They were men, and they couldn't help a little chest beating here and there. She'd allow them that much.

However, she was a woman, and, she believed, a member of the smarter sex. She also considered herself more grounded in reality. She couldn't let them think they were in complete control of these sexual escapades.

She looked down at Matthew's cock, holding back the smug smile that begged to show itself when that glorious organ reacted predictably to her scrutiny. She licked her lips, and just as she thought it would, his cock nodded at her.

As soon as his penis stretched above the water, she bent over in one smooth move and took him into her mouth.

"Jesus!" Matthew hissed in air between his teeth. He surged his hips, giving her more of his cock. His unexpected motion nearly knocked her off the bench and down into the tub.

The next moment, Steven's strong hands bracketed her hips, lifting her, easing her back. Matthew rose from the water at the same time, and in a matter of seconds, control of the situation had deftly been taken out of her hands as Steven set her on his lap.

"Yeah." Matthew combed his fingers through her hair, his hand cupping the back of her head. He began to thrust his hips, a light motion that Kelsey tried to control. She soon found she couldn't.

Steven eased her off his lap. Matthew inched back, leaving Kelsey standing, bent over at the waist. Matthew's left hand joined his right, and she felt captured by him, his hand guiding her head while he moved his cock in and out of her mouth.

Steven used one hand to caress the folds of her pussy even as she felt him reach out with the other. She'd felt him harden beneath her and knew he wanted her again.

She heard the tear, the glide. He brushed his latex-covered penis over the tiny opening to her anus. Kelsey felt everything inside her turn hot. Her body clenched, as if grabbing the sudden flare of arousal and holding it close. A groan escaped her throat completely without her permission.

"Oh, baby, you *liked* that." Steven's voice sounded strained. "Don't worry, we'll prepare you properly, but right now…"

He said nothing more, just impaled her cunt with his cock.

Oh, God. Kelsey loved the taste of Matthew's cock, the feel of it sliding in and out of her mouth. She loved the feel of Steven's cock buried deep in her pussy. They fucked her in tandem, their movements smooth, rhythmic. Kelsey played her tongue along Matthew's cock, one hand sliding down to cup his balls while her mouth gave him tiny little sucks. At the same time, she squeezed her inner muscles, caressing the cock that took her from behind, squeezing him so that he groaned and gripped her hips even harder.

"Drink me," Matthew said as his cock got hotter and harder.

She felt that first twitch and nearly hummed in pleasure because drinking him was precisely what she wanted to do.

Then Steven bent over her and found her clit with two fingers. He found it, captured it, and pinched it at the same moment Matthew began to come in her mouth.

Kelsey swallowed and came in a flood of fast, slithery spasms, the waves of orgasm feeling like tiny electric shocks cascading all through her body. The power of this climax rocked her, stealing her energy, her thoughts, until she became a creature of feeling, of nerve endings and stimulation and consummation. She swallowed and swallowed, every part of her wanting nothing more than to give and take and *feel*.

"Easy, sweetheart."

She didn't know who said that. Steven held her as he eased back so he sat once more on the submerged bench. Matthew bent over in front of her, his hands on his knees as he struggled for breath. Then he stepped forward, cupped her face in the same way his brother had earlier, and kissed her.

His lips felt warm and wet, even though the kiss itself seemed reverent.

"We're going to dry you off and tuck you in between us. You'll sleep here, with us, tonight," Matthew said.

A part of Kelsey's mind thought that maybe it would be better if they just had sex and went their separate ways when they were finished. Spending the night together implied an intimacy beyond the physical. Unfortunately, she couldn't get that part of her to speak up.

With ridiculous ease, the men bathed her, dried her, and carried her to the bed. The last thought she had before sleep claimed her was that she floated on a heavenly cloud, tucked in between two devils.

* * * *

Kelsey pulled herself out of the trance-like state she'd slipped into and brought her attention back to the task at hand. It was time for her to stop these mental meanderings and act like the responsible adult business owner she knew herself to be, rather than indulging in silly daydreams like some lackadaisical employee.

Her gaze tracked across the room to Tracy, whose attention appeared totally fixed on her morning routine of preparing the pasta salad du jour.

See? That's what you need to do too. You don't see Tracy gazing off into la-la land.

Kelsey focused on the ingredients on the counter and the pot waiting to receive them and pushed everything else out of her mind.

Today was Friday, and Friday's soup du jour was chicken vegetable. She'd tried offering a New England style clam chowder shortly after she'd opened, but the townsfolk's tastes didn't run overmuch to sea food. So she'd settled on less exotic fare and now could pretty much count on selling out of her soup, even in the hottest part of the summer.

Kelsey's mind wandered again. Her eyes landed on the vase of flowers tucked into the corner of the kitchen.

I should move those into my office so they won't distract me.

Kelsey felt her expression soften into a smile.

She couldn't stop thinking about the events of last night. She'd fallen asleep between Matthew and Steven, so exhausted she'd dropped off like a stone. Sometime around three in the morning, she'd been awakened. First, Steven had gathered her close, kisses and caresses leading to slow, gentle sex. Then, not long after, Matthew had rolled her on top of him, and she'd indulged herself in tasting every bit of him. That had led to faster, not-so-gentle sex.

When they'd driven her back to her apartment just shy of seven a.m., they'd asked to see her again tonight.

She could no more refuse them than she could stop breathing.

Kelsey shook her head. She supposed she could be excused for her lack of mental discipline. Considering that she'd had six orgasms last night after having none at all for more than five years...

Oh my God. Six orgasms in one night.

Until it happened to her, she would have sworn such a thing to be humanly impossible.

She turned her attention back to soup making and the conclusion she'd been coming to in her thoughts. More than likely the passion of the night before owed its existence to her long sexual drought.

She had no doubt whatsoever that given just a bit more time, and another night like the one just passed, her hormones would settle down. Then the reality of spending the night in the arms of two lovers at the same time would lose its heady appeal.

"Are you too busy for a visit?"

Kelsey smiled as the familiar voice of her best friend preceded her into the kitchen. Susan Benedict had been Kelsey's college roommate. At first meeting, they'd clicked. They'd kept in touch after graduation, and Susan had come to visit her in Austin when Sean had been born.

She'd been there, too, in the aftermath of tragedy, helping her get through the funerals, nagging her to get on with her life when each successive anniversary of that event arrived.

Kelsey had finally given in to her friend's nagging and moved to Lusty and opened her own restaurant.

Thank God for Susan and her nagging.

"I'm never too busy for you." Kelsey said, giving her best friend a huge smile.

Susan and Tracy exchanged greetings, then Susan came over to where Kelsey worked.

Looking at her now, Kelsey said, "You have the look of Sarah Benedict."

Susan's smile was one of the nicest things about her. Her entire face lit up with it, and her eyes sparkled.

"Everyone in my family has said that to me all my life. I heard you finally visited the museum yesterday. Of course," she lowered her voice and stepped closer, "that's not all I heard you did yesterday...or I should say, last night?"

Oh, hell. How had Kelsey allowed herself to forget that Matthew and Steven were Susie's brothers? She had just had sex with not one, but *two* of her best friend's brothers!

"Um, yeah. About that."

Susan burst out laughing. Then she threw her arms around Kelsey and hugged her tight. "I'm so happy for you."

Those words, whispered, shouted to Kelsey's conscience and her mindset that what she and the brothers Benedict had was only physical.

She put the last of the ingredients into the stock pot, covered it, and set it to simmer. She turned to look over at Tracy, who'd turned her attention back to work.

"We're going to my office. Holler if you need anything."

"No problem, boss. You want me to go ahead and start the roasts of beef when I'm done this?" Tracy asked.

"Yes, please. Three should be enough, don't you think?" The roasts were a good size, more than six pounds apiece. One of the Friday night favorites for the patrons of Lusty Appetites were the smothered roast beef sandwiches.

Tracy frowned, and Kelsey knew she was thinking. "We might get a bigger dinner crowd than usual. I've heard a lot of talk about that new space movie that opened up over at the Galaxy in Waco yesterday. Folks heading in to catch the early show may stop here to eat first."

Kelsey nodded. "Okay, make it four. We can always do something with the leftover for tomorrow's lunch."

Tracy smiled, and Kelsey understood it was in response to Kelsey's having acted on her input.

"My cousin seems to be working out," Susan said as they entered Kelsey's office.

"She is. She loves the work, and she has a real knack for it. As much as I'd hate to lose her, I'm going to try and convince her to take some formal training. She could become a fine chef in her own right and have her own place one day, if she wants to."

Kelsey opened the small fridge she kept in her office and handed Susan a bottle of water. Taking one for herself, she sat down behind her desk, unscrewed the cap, and drank.

"So. You went out with my two favorite brothers last night."

Since Susan was grinning like a fool, Kelsey relaxed. "Um, we didn't exactly *go out*."

"I kind of figured that. Where did they take you?" She scrunched her eyes for a moment, then blinked. "Oh, of course. To the ranch."

"I hope you're not going to ask me for a play-by-play because I am *not* dishing on sex with your big brothers."

Susan made a face. "Don't worry. I don't need any details."

"Well, that's a relief."

"Necessarily."

Kelsey laughed, the absurdity of the situation tickling her. "You know, if we were male, and I was seeing one or both of your sisters, you'd probably feel duty bound to bust my chops."

"Yeah, but see? That's where we women are so superior to the male of the species."

"Uh-huh." Not very eloquent, but in light of the way she'd behaved last night, Kelsey wasn't feeling particularly superior at the moment.

"I've known for a while they had their eye on you. Should I have said something, given you a heads-up?"

Kelsey played with the condensation on her water bottle while she sorted through her thoughts. Unaccustomed as she was to opening up to most people, it had surprised her, right from their first meeting, that she'd been able to confide in Susie.

"I don't think I even really *saw* them until a few weeks ago, if you know what I mean. Then they began to stop by for coffee, and we'd chat, first one, then the other. I thought they were vying for my attention, you know, a kind of sibling rivalry sort of thing."

"Maybe I should have filled you in on the family history, then." Susan's frown caught at Kelsey's heart.

"I don't think I was ready to see that, either."

"So…we're fine? I don't want you to think that I asked you to move here to Lusty to set you up or anything."

"No, we're fine. That is, as long as you're okay with the fact that I'm using your brothers as my own personal sex objects."

For one moment, Kelsey thought she saw a look of concern settle in Susan's eyes, but then the other woman blinked, and only laughter lurked there.

"They're big boys. They can take care of themselves."

Big boys. Yes, they certainly were. Kelsey felt her face color as she put another meaning entirely on that expression. Since Susan immediately seemed to be enthralled with her own water bottle, she guessed the double entendre had registered with her, too.

"I'm seeing them again tonight," Kelsey said. "I—" She wanted to be able to talk to Susan about them, she realized. *At least she won't even blink about my being with two men.* "I used to think that I'd never have sex again."

"I know. You said the therapist told you when you were ready your libido would awaken again."

"Yes, and I didn't believe her." Then, because this was her best friend and she didn't want her operating under any misconceptions, she said, "I'm ready for this. I need it, but it will never develop into anything permanent. I haven't changed my mind about that. I'll never fall in love again and certainly never get married again."

"This is the new millennium," Susan said. "Women don't have to fall in love or marry their lovers in this day and age. We're free and independent creatures."

When Kelsey tilted her head to consider that, Susan laughed. "Like I said, they're big boys. I'm sure they're not interested in hearts and flowers, either. And, as long as everyone is having a good time, what's the harm?"

Kelsey couldn't have agreed more. Her focus was only on the physical. As she took a good drink from her bottle of water, she refused to think about why Susan's assertion of her brothers' intentions seemed to dig at her heart.

Chapter 6

Matthew rolled the window down as he drove his pickup truck away from the center of town en route to the ranch. Early afternoon on a Friday in the middle of summer, and the streets of Lusty, Texas, had turned quiet. Of course, for the most part the streets of Lusty were always quiet.

He shook his head because the image of the young man he'd been popped into his thoughts. When he'd lit out of here headed for Chicago at the tender age of twenty-one, all he wanted was to leave quiet—and family tradition—behind. He'd wanted busy, bright lights, and action.

Now Matthew wanted nothing more than to stay here in Lusty, settle down, and raise a family.

Grandma Kate always liked to say that things happened in their own time and in their own way. He couldn't deny the truth of that as he thought about how his life had gone so far and especially when he thought about the arrival of Kelsey into his world.

There was no doubt in his mind that Kelsey Madison was the woman meant for Steven and him. He'd known it the first time he'd laid eyes on her.

She'd seemed so fragile the day she came into the restaurant to have her first look at the place. He'd felt a special kind of awareness the moment she'd walked through the door. One look at Steven, who'd been helping him finish up the painting and getting the restaurant ready for her, and he knew his brother had felt that instant connection, too.

He'd already known a bit about her past. The moment Susan suggested leasing the building at 32 Main Street to Kelsey, he'd done a thorough background check on her.

What he'd learned had not only broken his heart, it had put him on cautious alert. A woman with the kind of emotional baggage Kelsey carried would need special care.

Perhaps it had been a by-product of how he'd been raised with two dads and one mom, or maybe it was the family tradition of ménage marriages, but he considered women, *all* women, special, deserving of care and attention.

His instincts about her had proven true when, for the first several months, she hadn't even seen either Steven or him as men.

Thinking about last night brought a wide smile to Matthew's face. She sure as hell thought of them as men now.

He turned into the laneway of the ranch, drove on straight past the house to the barn. He knew his brother would be around the place. A creature of habit, Steven used Friday afternoon to fix any machinery or tack that needed repairs or worked around the house and yard performing upkeep.

Steven greeted him as he entered the saddle barn. "You on what they call bankers' hours these days, bro? Good thing you're going to be moving back here soon. You need to remember what it is to work for a living."

A soft snort and puff of air caught his attention. He didn't answer Steven right away, instead heading over to one of the stalls on the west side of the barn. As he approached, the palomino filly in that stall began to nod her head up and down, as if to tell him it was about time he'd made an appearance.

"Hey, Duchess. There's my girl." Matthew stroked the mare, a horse he'd had for more than six years. He made it a point to come out to the ranch and ride at least twice a week.

Once things were settled and he was living here again, he'd be able to do that more often. And, he conceded mentally, help out more with ranch work.

"Not my fault the sheriff's office has a summer schedule. I get Friday afternoon off, as well as Tuesday morning. Then all day Sunday. So not quite bankers' hours. Jealous?"

"Of a job in town? Hardly. You want to talk here or out there?" Steven nodded toward the range.

Matthew smiled. "Out there. Just let me toss a blanket on my lady here and grab a halter and some reins. We'll be good to go."

Before long, he and Steven were setting a brisk pace as they rode out away from the house and barn, deeper onto Benedict land. He loved these times, times when it was just him and his brother, the horses, and the land.

Matthew looked over at his brother, at the look of contentment on his face. Steven's heart was in the ranch while his was in police work. Because they'd been there together yesterday and because he'd not visited his great-greats at the museum in some time, Matthew's thoughts turned to the first Benedicts to ride this range. When he let his gaze take in the land, unchanged in the last century or so, he could imagine being back with his ancestors, with Caleb and Joshua as they took over a spread that had first been amassed by a man whose soul had been as black as sin.

"I wonder if they had to step cautiously with Sarah?" Steven asked, proving they were both on the same page. He brought his black gelding, Night Shadow, to a walk and turned, giving his attention to Matthew.

"Some, I imagine. I recall reading Joshua's journal. They believed her married when they met her, which made things difficult all the way around, considering they both fell in love with her almost at first meeting."

"I remember reading that, too. Even as they dealt with that small matter of eluding an assassin, it seemed as if they clicked right from the start."

"Of course," Matthew said, "we've never been allowed to read Sarah's journal, so we don't know the entire story."

Another family tradition was that the men were forbidden to read the journals of Sarah Benedict and Amanda Jessop-Kendall. Those were held in trust by the females of the family, and to date, none of them had ever shared much with their men.

"Maybe we can get Kelsey to answer that question for us one day," Steven said.

"Maybe we can."

"You certainly read her right," Steven said after a moment. "You said she'd agree to sex, call it that, and try to keep things between us only physical."

"I can hardly blame her, really. How many times has she said she's not looking to become involved with anyone?" Matthew shrugged his shoulders. "Every time we've asked her out, and anytime one of our well-meaning female relatives have tried to play matchmaker, that's how often. She's going to need time to accept what she already feels for us. To admit she's more than attracted, that she's already half-way in love with us would be, I imagine, a little like saying goodbye to her husband all over again."

"Hell of a thing," Steven said. "Lucky that bastard who murdered her husband and son was killed by the cops. Otherwise, we'd have to kill him."

Matthew didn't feel the need to comment, as once again, they were on the same page. If there was one thing Benedict men were known for, it was putting their woman front and center in their lives.

"I thought we'd eat here tonight," Steven said. "We can do up a stir-fry, impress her with our culinary expertise."

Matthew laughed. "Sounds good. Of course, we can't tell her the stir-fry is the only indoor cooking we can do."

"Probably won't need to. Her being a chef and all, she's bound to figure it out."

"Too bad we can't court her properly like we want to," Matthew said. "We'll have to save that for *after* we're married."

"After the way she balked at the bit of romance we gave her last night, I believe you're right." Steven looked out over the horizon, his eyes taking in their heritage. "Good save there, by the way."

"Thanks," Matthew said. "I kind of expected that would be her attitude when she acted all businesslike at the museum. Felt like she'd agreed to think about buying our used car rather than making love with us. Of course, her attitude only leaves us with that one alternative."

Steven nodded his head. "Fuck her brains out at every opportunity so she becomes addicted to us. And hope in the process her heart prods her to admit she loves us."

"Shouldn't take long," Matthew said. He reined his horse in, turning the mare toward home. "I'm already addicted to *her*."

"Yeah. That makes two of us."

* * * *

Kelsey had made one change to the plans for tonight. As she waited for Lusty's one and only stoplight to turn green, she thought back over the conversation she'd had with Steven earlier that afternoon. She'd expected some sort of argument when she'd told him she wanted to drive out to the ranch herself rather than have them pick her up.

She frowned, tapping her fingers on the steering wheel. He hadn't given her any argument at all, but he *had* talked her into coming earlier. Then he'd told her that since she cooked all day, he and Matthew would throw together some dinner for them.

Since he hadn't argued about her driving—so she could leave as soon as they were done instead of staying the night—she hadn't argued about arriving early and letting the men cook. It had meant leaving Tracy to close up, but she'd done that before, and really, what was the point of owning her own business if she couldn't take advantage of being the boss once in a while? The light turned green, and Kelsey's thoughts returned to tonight's agenda. So, okay, they'd have dinner first. It wasn't as if the three of them were having a date. The body had to eat, and they might as well do it together, and then move right on to the recreation portion of the night's program.

Probably roast chicken or stir fry, the ever-easy man-meal.

Kelsey drove through town, headed for the state road that led to the ranch. She passed what everyone called the Big House and, right across the street, what they referred to as the New House. That second mansion, home to the Jessop-Kendall family, had been built more than a century ago. Of course, it was built after the Big House, hence its name. Kelsey shook her head. She supposed she'd eventually get used to the way Texans thought. Since she'd lived in the state for nearly ten years already, she wondered when that would be exactly.

As she drove, her mind recalled some of the photos she'd seen at the museum the day before. Now that she thought about it, she realized there were several families in Lusty that had ménage relationships in them.

I wonder why I didn't notice that before?

If, before yesterday, she'd been asked to describe her new home town in one word, that word would have been "welcoming."

Being a newcomer and opening a new business in a small town where so many folks were related or could trace their roots back generations to the beginning of the town was usually a recipe for failure. Small towns sometimes tended to be xenophobic, treating outsiders like outsiders for years, if not decades.

Yet, from day one, her restaurant had been full, and people had been nothing but kind to her. At first, she'd attributed that to the fact they all knew she was "Susie's friend." Now she wondered if being the place it was, with people living alternate lifestyles, that simply meant everyone was more tolerant and accepting by nature.

She turned into the long, winding lane of the Benedict Ranch. She'd made the right decision, driving herself here. The short commute had done wonders in lifting the minor stress of the day, making her feel as if she'd just got her second wind.

She crested the small hill and smiled when the house came into view. It was just so pretty, that white two-story home with its green trim, wrap-around verandah and Grecian pillars.

Talk about pretty sights.

The two very buff and extremely handsome men standing on that verandah waiting for her certainly qualified as that.

She pulled her car up to just in front of the house. This close, she could see the men's expressions, even the color of their eyes.

It wasn't the sparkling blue of Matthew's eyes or the deep chocolate of Steven's that drew her. It was the heat, the expression of arousal and, if she wasn't mistaken, raw, naked intent they both wore. That look acted like a magnet and pulled her from the isolation of her vehicle.

They held their ground—or rather, their verandah—and Kelsey didn't know whether to approve that move or not. She couldn't accuse them of crowding her exactly. And they could point out, if they had a mind to, that she was the one who'd driven from town, and she was the one who now walked, one step at a time, toward them.

Why am I thinking in adversarial terms?

Perhaps her subconscious understood the situation better than she knew. Maybe, when it came right down to it, these men posed a danger to her she'd not quite reckoned upon.

"What's the matter, darlin'?" Steven's deep drawl brushed a tremor against her skin. Kelsey tilted her head to the side, her eyes searching and her mind scrambling to find an answer to the question. She'd come to a halt just shy of the steps leading up to them.

"I don't know. I just…I just felt skittish all of a sudden, as if I was on the precipice of something for a moment."

"We would never hurt you," Matthew said. His words, as had his brother's, shivered through her. She had a sense of something, something big and deep and necessary. And then that sense evaporated. She felt silly. She was being silly.

"I know." She inhaled deeply. Whatever else was or was not happening here, she did know that. These men would move heaven and hell to protect her, to take care of her. A part of her mind reasoned they'd do as much for any woman they took to their bed, and she believed that.

She also thought that what they were building between the three of them meant she somehow was special to them, and she believed that, too.

She didn't want to have anything beyond the physical, really. On the other hand, she wanted to matter to them, and she believed she did.

"Then come here," Steven said. "We've been patient waiting for you. But we need to touch you and kiss you and say hello."

Kelsey felt her smile widen. Steven wasn't one to spend too much time talking. Of the two brothers, he seemed the quietest. Matthew could talk a virgin out of her underwear. Steven would crook his finger, and she'd drop them gladly.

Kelsey was no virgin, and she felt the double-barrel impact of the brothers Benedict in every part of her body.

Just hearing Steven's stated intentions already had her nipples hard and her pussy wet.

She inhaled deeply, settled her inner voices, and went to them.

Chapter 7

Waiting for Kelsey to take those few steps up to him was the hardest thing Steven had ever done. He wanted to scoop her up and carry her to bed where he and his brother could just *plunder*. Energy sizzled through him, and he didn't have to look at Matthew to know it was the same for him.

He could see a similar awareness dancing through Kelsey, too. One look in her pretty green eyes and he knew she felt the air change around them, though she likely had no idea why.

Steven figured the universe gave off some kind of signal when mates came together. Had to be because that was exactly the sensation rolling through him.

"I thought about you all day," he said when she came nearer. She took one more step forward, and he reached for her, brought her all the way forward until her body nestled flush against his.

"Hello, Kelsey." He covered her mouth with his, needing to take her taste into himself more than he needed his next breath. He needed to begin the feasting that would sate his appetite. She tasted better than ripe peaches. Stroking his hands across her back and down to her luscious ass, he cupped her and brought her hips even closer, ensuring she felt her affect on him. His tongue explored her mouth, sweeping inside, brushing against her teeth, until he felt the tension in her let go, until she used her tongue to taste him in turn.

Despite his cock already being hard and getting harder with each second, he eased back from her. When she opened her eyes, blinked as if regaining her senses, he leaned in and gave her a chaste kiss on her nose.

"Hello yourself." Her distracted tone made him smile. She thought what they shared was only physical? Not hardly.

"My turn."

Matthew's voice drew her attention, and Steven watched as his brother gathered her in and laid his lips on hers.

A sense of rightness settled on him, and it was a sense he'd at one time despaired of ever feeling. Years ago, when Matt had left Lusty, Steven had felt certain he'd be back after only a few months. Then those months had turned into years, and *then* Matthew had married Linda.

At the time, he'd truly wanted his brother to be happy, even though he himself felt devastated. All his life he'd had dreams of the future, and those dreams had always included him and Matthew married to the same woman.

Finally, his world had come right. It thrilled him that Kelsey responded as hotly to Matt as she did to him.

Matthew took a step back from Kelsey, then flashed her the same smile that had always gotten him out of trouble. "I guess we should feed you first, before we gobble you down."

"Hey, I might be the one who does the gobbling," she said.

Steven laughed. "Yeah, you may very well be. Same goes, though. We should all eat."

He noted the way she made sure neither of them held her hand as they entered the house. A quick look over at his brother and it was all he could do not to laugh out loud. Matthew had noticed her quasi-withdrawal and was going to respond to it in the same way he was going to—by pretending not to notice it at all.

Last night, they'd come inside and gone straight up the stairs to the master bedroom. Remembering the night before, he'd felt certain Kelsey would have pressed him when he'd told her the bedroom wasn't his yet. It was the master bedroom, intended to be shared by him, his brother, and their wife.

What would Kelsey think if she found out they'd had it redecorated two months ago, using colors they knew she liked?

That was a question to be saved for a much later time.

"We kind of rushed you in and up last night, sweetheart. So how about the nickel tour now?"

He could see it on her lips. Part of her wanted to decline. After all, she wasn't here to inspect the home or comment on the furnishings. She was here for sex, pure and simple.

He knew another part of her, the part he knew had already more than half fallen for them, wanted to see where he lived and examine their tastes in decorating.

He'd not known many women who could turn down the offer of a house tour. He figured it was something in them, some genetic coding under the general heading of the nesting instinct that came to the fore.

Of course, the nesting instinct in her won. "All right, yes. I'd like to see your house."

This was the home he'd grown up in, and now it was *his* home. Other members of the family occupied different houses, some held in the family for generations. His folks had moved back to the Big House, and when she was in Lusty and not traveling all over hell's half acre, Grandma Kate lived with them. Susan had a room there, but she also kept an apartment in the fourplex she owned over on Elm Street.

Joshua and Alex, his other brothers, each had a house in town. They'd been talking lately of building a new place together on the outskirts. They wanted a house they could share with the woman of their dreams.

They never doubted they'd eventually meet her, and that certainty was a family tradition, too.

Steven took pride in his home. Much of the furniture was as it had been through his youth. His grandparents had bought big, expensive leather and wood pieces made to last. Because they intended to make this their family home together, he'd consulted his brother on every renovation. Their tastes had meshed, which had been a blessing. They'd hired a decorator for some parts, but he and Matthew had refurbished the master bedroom themselves. They'd also done the den. They didn't watch a lot of television, but when they did, they both wanted to enjoy the experience. The LCD screen they'd bought was the biggest Steven had ever seen. Judging from Kelsey's reaction, it was for her, too.

"Holy cow, everything in this house is big!" Kelsey immediately blushed when she said that.

Steven met her gaze for a long moment and then said, "The beds in the guest rooms are a standard queen size." There, let her see what she did with that.

"I see."

Like hell. If she had asked why the bed in the master bedroom was larger, then, he could have explained it was meant to be shared by three. Steven smiled and then continued the tour on into the kitchen.

"Oh, my God, this is gorgeous!"

They'd had the granite countertop imported from Canada and chosen large rectangular ceramic tiles for the floor. Both surfaces shimmered in shades of autumn brown and, the decorator had said, contrasted well with the pure white, hand-carved wooden cabinets they'd had installed.

He'd chosen to have a center work island in the midst of the room as he liked the look of it. And, while he didn't do a lot of cooking in this room, those who did told him he'd chosen the spacing and set-up well.

He smiled as Kelsey inspected all the drawers, looked in the oven, and cooed over the dishes in the cabinet.

"I guess it would be sexist of me to say this kitchen is wasted on a bachelor who rarely cooks." She grinned as she said that. Matthew laughed, and Steven only shrugged.

"I had to figure Susan would have told you neither of us cook much. And it's okay, you can be sexist. I *don't* cook here often, but aunts and cousins and my mom do from time to time. They like it."

"What's not to like?" Kelsey finished her inspection, then perched herself up on one of the leather stools that lined the island on one side.

"Okay, I'm ready to watch others cook my dinner."

"Hope you like stir-fry," Matthew said.

"I do. And I like roast chicken, too. "

Steven wondered if she was laughing at them, just a little. And he decided it was fine if the answer to that was yes. If she could laugh at them, she had to feel at ease with them. Whether she realized it or not, Ms. Kelsey Madison had taken a step away from "sex only" and toward a full-fledged relationship.

* * * *

Kelsey could hardly believe it, but touring Steven's home and sitting in the kitchen bantering while the two men prepared dinner felt more intimate than sex had the night before. She began to suspect that she may have bitten off more than she could chew with these two Benedicts.

She sipped the wine Steven had poured, a crisp Chablis that was one of her favorites, and took a moment to search her emotions.

While the moment felt intimate, it didn't feel threatening. She was still captain of her ship, in charge of her destiny, and that destiny had been carved in stone.

She might hook up with the male of the species from time to time in order to play, but she'd live the rest of her life alone.

"I think you qualify for some sort of award," Matthew said.

Kelsey tilted her head slightly. "For what?"

"Making no comment so far on our technique."

She set her glass down and used two fingers to gently turn it as she considered all the possible responses she could give him.

"Well, in fairness, I *was* going to wait until I got dressed again later before giving either of you a score. Last night might have been a fluke."

"Smart ass," Steven said.

She watched as he began to sear the beef strips in the wok. Matthew finished chopping the vegetables, then checked the rice in the steamer. The kitchen filled with the smell of food, and as always, even when it wasn't her own food, Kelsey took a moment to close her eyes, inhale deeply, and appreciate the aromas.

She opened her eyes to encounter the two men treating her to identical heated gazes.

"There should be a rule about distracting the cooks," Matthew said.

"I agree." Steven put his attention back on the wok.

"I have no idea what you're talking about. I was simply…enjoying the scents."

It had been a long, long time since Kelsey had allowed herself the freedom to flirt. When Matthew speared her with another stare, she said nothing, simply batted her eyelashes.

"Us, too, come to that. You smell sultry, savory, and sexy."

"Ooh, alliteration. Be still my heart."

"You know," Steven said conversationally, "smart asses run the risk of being spanked around here."

"You might call that another family tradition, one that's not spoken of very often," Matthew added.

The air fairly crackled with sexual tension. Kelsey felt it along her arms and legs, then spiraling deep into her, settling low in her belly. Her nipples tightened and her pussy gushed. She'd never been spanked in her entire life. She didn't know what to think about the fact that the mere mention of the possibility of a spanking had her dripping with horniness.

They seemed to understand how their words had affected her, too, because they'd traded a look she couldn't completely read.

She cleared her throat. "Is that right? So, would that be like a round-robin sort of activity?"

"Certainly not. Any Texan will tell you only women can be smart asses and earn spankings. The similar quality in a man is merely referred to as wit."

"There sure are a lot of rules in Texas," Kelsey said. She'd aimed for a light, breezy tone, but it emerged more of a breathless one.

"That's because Texan men pride themselves on their attention to detail," Steven said without looking up from the stove.

"We do, indeed," Matthew agreed. "And one such little detail demands that we ask you which you prefer, honey or chocolate?"

"Honey or chocolate what?"

"Sauce. Your being a chef opens up a world of gourmand possibilities for us. So, which would you prefer to have us lick off every inch of your body? Honey or chocolate?"

"What, no strawberry?" *Oh my God, I don't believe I just said that.* Kelsey's heart pounded in her chest in response to the expression on the brothers' faces.

"We thought we'd save the strawberries for our own unique version of bobbing for apples," Steven said.

"Mmm, I can nearly taste how sweet those berries are going to be as I tongue them out of your pussy," Matthew said.

Kelsey forgot how to breathe. The picture these men painted acted like tinder on her already smoldering libido. She picked up her glass of wine, downing the contents in one toss, not even taking a moment to enjoy the tang of the grape on her tongue. Her mind threw her incendiary images of her and these two rogues enacting every single scenario they'd mentioned.

Her appetite for food diminished in direct proportion to the increase in her hunger for them.

They exchanged a look, these brothers who seemed bent on driving her out of her mind. Then Matthew unplugged the rice steamer and Steven turned off the stove.

"Sandwiches, later," Matthew said. He reached out to her, his fingers working quickly to unfasten the buttons of her blouse. Steven moved behind her, pressing himself against her from behind. She could just feel the imprint of his cock against the small of her back, and she wondered at the speed with which they had all gone from the mundane to the sensual.

Kelsey had no more time to think. The moment the last button of her blouse came open, Steven whipped it off her while Matthew reached around behind her and opened her bra. Then he lifted her, and she felt Steven unbutton and unzip her skirt. It and her panties joined the rest of her clothing in a heap on the floor.

Her bare bottom hit the cold granite of the kitchen island. Matthew spread her legs as Steven eased her down so she lay stretched out before them, an offering at waist height.

Steven's mouth covered hers, his tongue hot and determined to taste all of her at once. One hand held her two wrists together, arms above her head. The other cupped her breast, tweaking and pulling at her nipple.

She became so lost in Steven's kiss, the sound of cupboards being opened and closed nearly didn't register. Then she felt the heat of Matthew's body standing between her legs once more.

His thumb stroked the bare skin above her clit just a split second before she felt something warm, wet, and thick land there.

Steven broke their kiss and shifted his gaze to watch his brother.

"I thought we'd start by making this a real honey pot," Matthew said.

Kelsey arched, whimpering with need as Matthew began to lick the sweet nectar from her flesh.

Chapter 8

Wesley Connors felt certain not even his bride would recognize him.

If Cora Lynn were sitting in this second-rate eatery in this Podunk little town, she wouldn't know it was her own husband who'd just walked in the door.

He'd been careful with his disguise, especially careful because, well, after this little problem had been resolved, his face would be splashed all over television screens and newspapers throughout the great state of Texas. He'd be easily recognizable then, so he needed to be extra careful now.

He'd gone to a costume supplier out of town and purchased body padding, and he'd worn a blond, long-haired wig, a mustache, and glasses when he'd done so. He'd paid cash for everything he'd bought.

Tonight, he'd donned that padding, the larger clothing he'd picked up to go with it, another wig, different glasses and a beard. Driving in the get-up had been a pain in the ass, but he felt confident as he sat down in Lusty Appetites that if anyone remembered him, they would only recall the disguise he wore.

Wesley's stomach growled in response to the aroma of food that permeated the air. He was here tonight on a reconnaissance mission, so his best course of action would be to order a meal.

He didn't have to wait long before a waitress appeared. She poured water into the glass at his table and handed him a menu so he could peruse the bill of fare.

Her smile was bright and sunny. He couldn't help but notice how sexy she looked in her simple white blouse and black skirt.

"Good evening and welcome to Lusty Appetites. I'm Michelle, and I'll be taking care of you this evening."

"Hello, Michelle." He figured if he didn't smile or talk, he'd stand out more in the woman's memory than if he did. Whenever he'd gone anywhere before he got married, he'd felt free to flirt with any woman who appealed to him. He'd had to curtail the habit, especially once he decided to run for mayor. It occurred to him that disguised as he was, there was no need to deny himself a little fun. Michelle certainly appealed to him. Her sleek blond hair and soft womanly curves looked like they'd give him a very comfortable ride. He lowered his voice and asked, "What looks good tonight?"

"Our Friday special is a smothered roast beef sandwich with lots of onions and gravy."

"That sounds really good." He closed the menu and gave her his best smile. "No need to read any further. I'll have that."

He sat back and waited for his food, keeping his attention focused so that every time the door to the kitchen opened, he peered inside. Once, he saw a young woman dishing up food, but she wasn't the woman he'd come there to see.

He remembered Kelsey Madison. For a couple of years after the incident, he'd sometimes seen her face front and center in his dreams.

His dinner was served promptly, and he had to admit the food tasted good. He could see why this place had been written up in the food section of the Waco paper.

He took his time eating, giving all the appearance of having nothing more on his mind than clearing his plate.

When the waitress returned to check on him, he raved over the meal. "The reason I came all the way here from Waco was because I saw that write-up in the Tribune-Herald last month."

"You know, we have a lot of people coming all the way from Waco because of that article."

"Well, it's certainly been well worth the trip." Then he frowned, as if trying to remember something. "The owner...Kelly, Kathy..."

"Kelsey. Kelsey Madison," Michelle said.

"Right! Kelsey! Is she available for a moment? My mamma raised me to always say thank you for the vittles. I'd like to tell Ms. Madison how wonderful my dinner was."

"Oh, that's so sweet of you! Unfortunately, this is Kelsey's early night, and she's already gone home, but I'll be sure to give her your compliments."

"Thanks, I appreciate that. The beef really was quite delicious."

"Nothing we like more than a satisfied customer. Now, can I tempt you with dessert and coffee?"

Because he needed to appear like a normal diner, he ordered the apple pie with ice cream and coffee.

It wouldn't do to ask, so he had to assume that Friday was Kelsey's regular early night. Actually, that could work to his advantage because Cora Lynn had a regular Friday lady's club meeting. Friday was the one evening he could come and go without worry of interference.

His gaze wandered to the window. There wasn't much traffic about, not many people in this dinky little town, actually. It shouldn't be difficult to follow the woman once she left work. Probably, it would be a good idea to come here and eat a few times, so if he was seen no one would bother about him. He could be a bit of a familiar face, especially when the face and body weren't really his.

Michelle delivered his coffee and dessert. "You know, we have a wonderful Sunday buffet, if that's something that would appeal to you. We serve it from two p.m. till eight every Sunday."

Wesley pretended to consider that. "Thanks. I'll see what I can do. This food is certainly worth a second trip."

Of course, Sunday was out of the question. He and Cora Lynn usually ate dinner at her parents' house on Sunday.

He took note of the hours. He'd see about fitting in a lunch through the week. He sipped his coffee, glanced around the eatery.

Now that he'd been here, confidence filled him. He could do this, no sweat. One bold move, then he would be free to get on with the rest of his life. He was certainly entitled to that.

* * * *

Kelsey wondered that she didn't shatter into a dozen tingling, pleasure-filled pieces.

Matthew used his tongue in long, lavish strokes to lap the honey from her body. He seemed in no hurry as he set about to drive her out of her mind, bringing that lovely organ so close to where she needed it most. He licked her labia and the delicate flesh above her clit. She swore she could feel that tiny nubbin stretch out of its protective hood, reaching for some of that oral play.

Kelsey let loose with an animal-like sound of frustration. Matthew responded with a soft chuckle against her moist skin and by placing one hand on her chest just below and between her breasts, as if holding her in place.

At that moment, Steven stepped away but returned to her quickly. Then she felt something wet plop onto her right breast, and the aroma of chocolate teased her senses.

"*Oh, God.*"

"Yum, chocolate-covered nipple." Steven swirled his tongue around the pebbled point, then sucked it into his mouth. The strong tug seemed to go deep inside her, down through her core, to tingle and pulse in her pussy.

She hadn't noticed that while he'd stepped away from her she'd left her arms stretched above her head, wrists together. Now he cuffed them again with one hand, sending her a look of male superiority— no, male *domination*—that spiked her arousal even higher.

She wanted to come. She wanted that deep plunge into bliss that these men had given her so many times the night before. She wanted to touch them, to taste them and pleasure them in any way, every way imaginable. She wanted to give and take and take and *take*.

How could she want and need so fiercely when she'd been so sated the night before?

"What's the matter, sweetheart?"

Kelsey looked down between her legs to encounter Matthew's gaze. One eyebrow raised, he looked every inch the arrogant male. His lips glistened wetly in the kitchen lights, and she realized it was her own nectar there.

"Kiss me." She needed to taste herself on his lips, to share the pleasure he took from her and gave to her in equal measure.

She saw the evidence of the heightened passion her words evoked. He moved over her in one smooth, deliberate move.

They tasted of lust and of desire. The salty, musky flavor of this kiss fed a need in her, a need that had lain dormant. Feral, basic, that need grew, as if now it would no longer be held back. He pressed his hips against her, and his stiff cock, covered in unforgiving denim, brushed against her clit, sending her over the edge into raw climax.

Kelsey screamed, everything inside her burning white hot, orgasmic, as the waves of rapture threatened to down her. Even in the haze of orgasm, she knew the men anchored her, held her, and she was safe.

"Oh, baby. Do you have any idea how hot it makes us when you respond so sweetly?" Matthew bathed her face with his words as he laid kisses on her cheek and neck. He eased back, lifting his chest from her, but stayed between her splayed legs, caressing them and the inside of her thighs.

"Your nipples just went rock hard." Steven caressed and pinched them. Kelsey whimpered, the small bite of pain bowing her off the counter, stirring her arousal to life once more.

"I want to touch you. Taste you. I want us all naked and rolling around on that enormous bed of yours."

Steven covered her mouth with his, his tongue possessing her, tasting her in a way she'd never known before these men kissed her.

"I can taste your cunt on your lips." His ragged whisper told her how close to the edge he'd come. "You have a flavor better than any food, any drink. I want more of it." He looked up at his brother, then nodded. "Yeah, let's move this party to the bedroom."

* * * *

She barely let Steven finish undressing before she reached for his cock. He was longer than his brother, not quite as thick, but just as mouth-watering. On the bed and on her knees, she'd stopped him in his tracks. He had one foot on the floor, a knee on the bed, and now, both hands in her hair as she sucked him deep.

Hot and salty, smooth and velvety, his cock fit her mouth as if it had been made for her. She moved on him, sliding her lips down his shaft, taking him deep, swirling her tongue along the veins she could feel.

Steven hissed his breaths. His fingers clenched, then held her head even more securely. His tension increased her lust. The knowledge that she pleased him, pleasured him, and drove him to hissing and clutching stroked her sense of power, her elemental woman.

Kelsey had the dim thought that her elemental woman had been shackled too long.

Then the bed dipped, and Matthew, hot, hard, and gloriously naked, cozied up to her, rubbed his throbbing cock against her shoulder, and ran his hand down her naked back.

Using her right hand, she fisted Matthew, stroked him slowly, firmly, and played her thumb against the small hole, spreading the viscous sign of his need.

"Tease."

Kelsey smiled at the one word challenge, but kept her mouth on
Steven's cock. She began to slide her lips down, taking as much as
she could, then backed up, nearly releasing him. Steven shuddered,
and she repeated the motion two more times. When she brought her
lips close to the head of his cock again, she released him, turned her
head, and immediately took Matthew into her mouth.

"Woman, you have a *great* mouth," Matthew said.

Kelsey began to suck him hard, making him groan. She brought
her head up, released him, then deep-throated his brother.

Back and forth she worked, one cock, then the other, marveling at
the different taste, the different texture, between these two brothers.

I'd be able to tell them apart, blindfolded, just from this.

And their scent. She inhaled each one deeply, just there at the base
of their cocks, where she could sample the compelling aroma of cock
and scrotum and man. Here, too, she found a difference, yet each
aroma, each flavor, thrilled and aroused her identically.

Kelsey didn't know where this primal, feral side of herself had
been hiding all her life. She only knew it had awakened now, and she
would greedily gulp down all the excitement, all the stimulation that
had been lacking for so very long.

She felt the men nearing their peaks and could already read the
telltale signs. Their breathing hitched, their eyes closed, and their
bellies had both gained a fine sheen of perspiration.

She sat back on her haunches, a hand around each cock, and
continued to stroke with an even slower, lighter touch.

"Now I'm a tease."

Two pairs of eyes opened, and two stares fastened on her as she
smiled back at them.

"I do believe you were warned what being a smart ass could get
you." Matthew raised one eyebrow, his expression arrogant. He
reminded her of a pirate with that roguish grin and that steely gaze he
could switch on and off at will.

"Maybe I didn't believe the warning. Maybe I've decided to tempt fate." She felt bold, reckless, and brazen. As that newly awakened part of her stretched and basked, Kelsey secretly rejoiced in the sense of freedom and fun that filled her. "Or maybe," she lowered her eyes, then looked up, letting her arousal show, "maybe I've decided to take you up on the offer."

"Careful. Little girls who tease horny men sometimes get more than they can handle."

Steven's words shivered down her spine and tickled the area deep in her belly that quivered with sexual excitement. She met his gaze and felt it sear her, as if he could see deep inside her. He'd looked at her like this for one moment down in the kitchen, that moment when he'd returned to her and she'd left her arms as if he'd held them still.

Matthew's hand stroked her hair, then settled on her shoulder, drawing her gaze to him. In his eyes she saw such heat and such hunger that everything feminine within her at once celebrated and trembled in apprehension.

An offer awaited just below the surface of their conversation. The brothers waited, said nothing, and Kelsey understood what did or did not happen next was completely up to her.

She nearly didn't recognize herself because such uninhibited desire filled her. No matter what she chose, it would be fine. She had complete freedom to dare or to turn away. All the power lay in her hands, and she'd never felt so seduced.

"I can handle you. Both of you. I want to take whatever you give me. I want it all."

Chapter 9

They moved so quickly Kelsey could barely catch her breath. One moment she'd issued the most daring challenge of her life, and the next she'd been stretched out on the bed, the two men on either side of her, one holding her wrists above her head, the other pinning her two legs beneath one of his.

"So, you want us to spank you. What else do you like? What other things would you have us do to you?" Matthew stroked his hand over her breasts, pausing just a moment to tweak her nipples, then smoothed his palm down her body, stopping just above her mound.

"We want to fulfill every one of your fantasies." Steven used a finger to trace her lips, then dipped it into her mouth to bring some of her moisture to them.

"I didn't know." They captivated her. Their touch was so arousing, so *necessary*, she could find no words to give them beyond that. Everything inside her felt ready to combust. She'd never been so aroused.

"You didn't know that you wanted us to spank you until now?" Matthew's voice turned tender, settling in her like something warm and comforting. An alarm bell sounded in her head, but she turned it off. She didn't want to think. She simply wanted to *feel*. Instead of answering him in words, she simply shook her head no.

"And you don't have any idea what all you might like, or need?" Steven's tone matched his brother's.

Again, she could do little more than shake her head.

"Well, now. I would say the possibilities for us are endless." Matthew leaned down and kissed her, a gentle, questing kiss that wooed her lips and teased her senses.

When he moved back, Steven moved in, his kiss just as light and just as intoxicating. "So we'll tell you what. Anything you can think of, we'll try. Anything *we* can think of, we'll try. And all you have to do at anytime is say stop. Does that work for you?"

Kelsey looked from one to the other. They wore equal expressions, a mix of tenderness and arousal. They were offering to make every one of her fantasies come true. They'd mentioned something before, something she never would have believed she could share with anyone, let alone have made real.

She swallowed hard. "I want…" Her heart pounded, and a delicious tremor nestled low in her belly. A few butterflies? More like a swarm of them. She licked her suddenly dry lips. Until now, she'd never let herself crave or demand. Here and now, craving and demanding weren't just allowed, they'd somehow become mandatory. "I want what you offered last night. I want the spanking, yes, but last night you said, both of you at once. I want both of your cocks inside me at the same time."

"You want one cock in your pussy and one in your ass?" Matthew's hand continued to stroke her, low on her belly and down her left leg. He moved so that he no longer pinned her but lifted her leg over his hip, opening her to their view. He held her in place so she couldn't hide herself even if she wanted to. Of course, a tiny part of her wanted to, but that side of her that cried out to do and explore and to live was getting louder and louder. Did she want the fantasy of double penetration to become real?

"*Yes.*" How could she tell them being taken that way had always been her secret fantasy? How could she tell them that when she had sexual dreams, they would be about that? Always in the past, the image would steal into her mind in the middle of the night. Two men, nameless, faceless, would arouse her, use her, in just that way. She'd always awaken in the middle of a fierce orgasm that somehow left her unsatisfied and with a sense that her dream had been naughty. Her fantasy felt naughty no more.

"Anything. Everything," Matthew said. In that instant, she could have wept with joy because they understood her.

This might be only sex, but there existed a connection here. They *got* her. That might be scary. She'd worry about that later.

Matthew reached up, cupped her face with one hand, and turned her head so their gazes met. "We won't hurt you, sweetheart. There may be just a bit of pain, a tiny bit to spice the arousal. It should never hurt. Do you understand? So if you want our cocks in your ass, we'll give them to you. In stages."

"In stages?" Kelsey wasn't insulted by the look of indulgent teasing that came into his eyes, nor the way he flicked his gaze to his brother.

"You have to be stretched first, baby," Steven explained. "We have toys."

Crinkling her nose, she said, "I hope you've sterilized them since the last time you used them."

Matthew roared with laughter while Steven just put his head down on her chest and chuckled silently.

"These are brand new toys, Kelsey, never before used. We went shopping a few weeks ago, online, with you in mind."

"Oh." It seemed too surreal that while she still had been unaware of their desire for her, they'd been thinking of her, of this, and had gone shopping for toys. She felt her face heat. She didn't want to feel embarrassed, and she didn't want to think. She knew of one sure way to avoid both.

"Less talking. More action."

"Yes, ma'am." Matthew appeared on the brink of laughter. She tried not to resent the way he could seem so unaffected, lying naked together on the bed like this. She felt as if she was going to come apart at the seams any moment, yet these men appeared—

Matthew speared two fingers into her, reaching deep, then spreading those fingers, fucking them in and out of her with strong, steady movements. He brushed against something inside her, and she came, an explosion of ecstasy so sudden and sharp she didn't get the chance to anticipate it. She could do nothing but let it batter her with wave upon wave of orgasmic bliss.

"You look so hot when you're coming." Matthew leaned down, kissed her, then shifted closer and changed the angle if his fingers inside her. "Wild and hot. Your eyes glaze, and your skin looks kissed by roses."

"Oh, God."

Steven had slithered down her body, placing wet, open-mouthed kisses on her left breast and down her side. When Matthew pulled his fingers out of her, Steven replaced them with his mouth.

He spread her wide, got up on his knees, then lifted her. She felt the impression of his hands on the cheeks of her ass, felt herself taken in hand at the same time his tongue began to caress and stroke her pussy. He wasn't coy about it, either, but licked and tasted with long, strong sweeps of his tongue. He found her clit, teased it, then sucked it into his mouth.

She'd left her arms over her head and now grasped the brass bars of the headboard. Noises of need—grunts, mews, and groans—erupted from her throat, and she felt as powerless to stop them as she was to control the riot of sensations sizzling all through her body.

Steven began to lap at her, lifting her so that his tongue started at the bottom of her slit, stroked up, and swirled against her clit. He did it again and then again. And then he brushed against the rosette of her anus, pushing his tongue in a little as he stroked over her, setting her ablaze.

Matthew moved on the bed beside her, but she couldn't spare him more than the barest notice because Steven opened his mouth over her cunt and began to suck.

"Oh, oh, oh!" A second orgasm captured her, lifted her from the ground and carried her high, higher into the clouds where there was nothing solid to grab on to, just the sense of soaring, sailing, with no end in sight.

Matthew moved and something smooth and cold brushed against her anus, pushed in, then releasing. Then something harder, larger, pressed against that virgin opening, pressing and pressing, and then sliding slowly into her.

Steven lowered her and moved up her body. She felt the brush of his latex covered erection against her wet folds. He sank in, balls deep in one sure thrust.

Kelsey wrapped herself around him, lifting her hips to receive him, the feeling of fullness, of being stretched and stuffed simply incredible.

She felt a hand stroke her head, and she turned, opened her mouth, and kissed Matthew.

"We'll keep that butt plug in you for a few hours," he whispered. He returned his mouth to hers, and Kelsey sucked his tongue deep. The slap of flesh, the grunt of one lover filling her, and the scent of their bodies all combined to push Kelsey over the edge once more.

This time she came and came and wondered how the world didn't explode in a giant ball of fire and consume them all.

* * * *

Matthew stood on the front porch, birdsong serenading him as he sipped from his mug of coffee. His gaze landed on Kelsey's car, and he grinned. He and Steven both knew she'd driven here last night so she could get out of bed and drive herself home. Staying over hadn't been her intention, as that action would seem to her to be just a bit *too intimate*.

Of course, she hadn't counted on their determination to love her so hard and so well that she'd have no choice but to sleep.

So far, their campaign to win Kelsey was going according to plan. She didn't miss an opportunity to reiterate that the relationship they'd embarked on was sex only. He and Steven always readily agreed with her, even as they worked to make it more than that.

To the east, the horizon grew lighter, pale pink streaked with faint yellow, daybreak gathering as if being created out of the mist. Steven had already headed out to the barn, and Kelsey slept on.

He'd rather she kept on sleeping. Before they'd brought her to their bed, he and Steven had both noticed she seemed to do little more in her life than work. She had made no room in her life for fun. He and Steven wanted to love her in every sense of the word, and that meant doing loving things like taking care of her, pampering her, and letting her sleep.

Of course they had to balance that against her wishes. Kelsey wouldn't appreciate their letting her continue sleeping when she had work to do. Saturday was one of the busiest days at Lusty Appetites, and he and Steven both respected her dedication and work ethic too much to try and interfere with that.

Maybe someday in the future, when her belly swelled round with their first child, they might suggest a lighter schedule.

Matthew sighed. They wanted to give Kelsey everything, including filling the hole in her mother-heart.

He couldn't imagine the pain she'd endured, watching her family gunned down before her very eyes. He recalled, when it happened, how Susan had been so completely devastated and so determined to do all she could for her good friend.

When she'd told the town trust she wanted to renovate a building on Main to be a restaurant for Kelsey, the vote had been a unanimous yes.

One look at Kelsey and Matthew and Steven had said a unanimous yes, too.

Winning Kelsey's love wasn't going to be easy, but sure as hell would be worth whatever trouble they had to go through—even letting the woman they loved function under the mistaken belief that they were only interested in sex with her.

The day grew lighter.

Time to go wake up our sleeping beauty with some fresh coffee and a kiss.

Next time, he'd head out to cover the chores and give Steven the privilege.

He found her as they'd left her, sprawled face down in the middle of the bed. She'd kicked the blankets down so that she lay prone, naked down to the cute little dimple above the crack of her ass.

He set the cup on the nightstand. Certainly awakening the woman he loved with fresh coffee, made to order, would be considered thoughtful by anyone's definition. Matthew definitely wanted to be considered thoughtful.

Then again, he'd also like to be considered lusty.

The town being named what it was and all.

Matthew grinned and dropped his clothes. Using a gentle hand, he pulled the sheet all the rest of the way off Kelsey. Asleep, she looked sweet and innocent. The soft play of her long lashes against her cheeks, the very light dusting of freckles across her nose, and the slight smile kissing her lips all came together to make one package that was simply irresistible.

His cock already bobbed against his belly, hot and hard and needy. He took a moment to grab a condom from the bedside table and roll it into place. Then he bent down over Kelsey and began to kiss her feet. He moved his tribute up her body, lips and tongue tasting her and slowly, so slowly, waking her.

"Mmm."

"That's my line. You're very, very tasty, Ms. Madison."

"Matthew."

His name had emerged on a breathless sigh and damned if that didn't make his cock even harder.

"Yes. Matthew." He said the words against that lovely little dimple.

"Steven?"

He didn't want to tell her his brother was likely out shoveling horse shit. So he only said, "Later."

He knelt on the bed, straddled her, and used one of his knees to part her legs. With his tongue, he caressed the crack of her ass, giving her flesh lavish attention as she moaned and squirmed.

He bit her ass, his bite not completely gentle, then licked away the sting. Apparently, she really liked that for she began to move her bottom, looking for more attention. Before long, she raised herself up onto her knees, a tiny whimper escaping her throat.

"Sweetheart, are you awake?"

"Yes."

"Good."

Matthew dipped then surged up, his cock brushing against her ass then sliding down and around until he caressed her pussy lips. One more nudge and his dick plunged all the way into her cunt.

"Ah!" She shivered and then moved, working her inner muscles to squeeze him while he began to thrust in her. Her hot, wet sheath felt so good. The rippling around his cock aroused him so much, he didn't know how long he could keep from coming.

"You feel so damn good." He bent down and placed tongue kisses against her neck and the shell of her ear, chuckling when she shivered in response.

"Please!" She raised herself right up on her knees, the needy sounds coming from her telling him how close she was to her own climax.

He rested his weight on her just a little and reached under her with one hand. He stroked her slit with his fingers, and she tilted her pelvis toward him. Her clit stood up, eager little thing, and he grabbed it between his forefinger and thumb and squeezed it gently.

"Come with me, baby. Let go and fly with me."

Her scream of completion pushed him over the edge. He slammed into her and held himself deep and tight against the bud of her cervix.

As he felt his seed explode from his body, he imagined, for one moment, that he filled her with life.

Chapter 10

"You sure have been smiling and humming lot in the last few weeks."

Kelsey looked up from the chicken and dumplings she was preparing for Lusty Appetite's Sunday buffet. Tracy had begun filling the cream puffs they'd made that morning with fresh whipped cream. It was nearly twelve-thirty. The restaurant opened for the Sunday buffet in just under two hours. In the corner, a radio turned to low volume played country hits.

Kelsey hadn't realized she'd been humming along with the radio, but now that Tracy mentioned it, she shrugged.

"I guess I have. Probably because I've been in a pretty good mood the last few weeks." That was nothing less than the truth. These last few weeks, she'd been feeling better rested than she had in years and more energetic, too. She almost felt...normal.

Tracy said, "I would be in a pretty good mood, too, if I was having regular sex with two incredibly hunky men."

When Kelsey felt her eyes go wide, Tracy laughed. "Yeah, I know they're family, sort of, but that doesn't mean I don't have eyes. Those particular Benedict brothers are Grade A Texas Prime."

Kelsey grinned. She certainly couldn't deny Tracy's assessment. Neither could she deny that sex with two hunky men likely accounted not only for her good mood but her sleeping better, too. Although she'd gone into this ménage relationship with a lot of pent-up sexual frustration, she'd had some doubts, as well. She'd doubted it would take long for her sexual appetite—never very huge at the best of times—to be sated. She'd doubted it would take long for the men in question to get tired of her, or tired of sharing her, or both. She'd doubted people would continue to look favorably on the three of them as time passed when it became known that they were all engaged in a sexual affair.

Yet here she was, nearly a month into, as Tracy put it, having regular sex with two hunky men, and not one of her doubts had proven out.

Since Tracy wore a teasing grin, Kelsey shrugged. "I highly recommend the activity."

"You don't have to sell me on the benefits of having two lovers. Although my parents are a single couple, my aunt and uncles are a threesome, and they're very happy together. As a matter of fact, I don't believe I've ever seen Aunt Pammy without a smile on her face or a bounce in her step."

"It doesn't seem strange to you? That so many families here in Lusty live alternate lifestyles?"

"Not at all. It's always been that way. Normal's just what you're used to," Tracy said.

Kelsey couldn't argue with her logic. Neither could she believe that she never noticed the proclivities of the locals to live as they did until she began having her affair with Steven and Matthew Benedict. The fact was that here in Lusty, Texas, families with just one husband and wife were the anomaly.

They both got back to work. Tracy put the first tray of cream puffs into the fridge and began work on another. The restaurant also offered several different pies in the dessert bar on Sundays. One of the ways the Lusty Ladies Auxiliary raised money for their civic projects was by selling fresh-baked pies to Lusty Appetites. This was a win-win situation as far as Kelsey was concerned. She not only received delicious pies for her restaurant, she could be guaranteed that on most Sundays many of those women's families came to eat, too.

"Will you be heading to the ranch again after closing?" Tracy asked.

"Mmm." Kelsey slid her tray of chicken into one oven and set the timer. She walked over to the sink, washed her hands, then checked the large pot of barbeque sauce she had simmering. Tonight's buffet would also feature pulled pork done in the rich sauce and the perennial favorite, prime rib roast beef.

Kelsey set right to bringing the roasts out of the fridge and preparing them for the oven. She realized she'd avoided answering Tracy's question. It was just that answering it would mean admitting she'd been spending a lot of time lately at the ranch. Looking back over the last few weeks, she couldn't say she'd spent more than three or four nights on her own in her own apartment. Of course, it made sense that if the three of them were getting together to have hot monkey sex they should do it in the one bed available to them that was big enough.

Even though she asserted at least once every few days that this relationship was just sex, and the men agreed with her, that wasn't how it was beginning to feel.

It was beginning to feel like a real relationship with real feelings and expectations and everything.

Well, of course there would be feelings. It's a good idea that I really like the men I entrust my body to.

True enough. Kelsey wasn't altogether certain the feelings she had for Steven and Matthew Benedict were *only* feelings of friendly affection.

"You know, when I was first hired on here," Tracy said, "I never thought I'd get used to having Monday and Tuesday off, but I have. I can still do all the things I used to do on Saturdays, but the places I go aren't as crowded."

"Yes, I think closing the restaurant Mondays so everyone can get at least one regular day off makes sense." She herself left early on Friday, and Sunday was a short day, only from eleven to about eight.

She looked over at Tracy and wondered if the other woman had somehow deliberately distracted her from thinking about her relationship with Steven and Matthew. Kelsey shook her head. *This was why she didn't give herself much time to think lately.* Her mind could come up with the damndest things. Like her friend and *sous-chef* could be devious enough to keep her from thinking too deeply about her lovers.

Or like trying to convince herself she had fallen in love with the brothers Benedict when they were all only friends—friends with benefits.

* * * *

Kelsey knew her staff was giving her sideways glances. She pretended not to notice, though, as she stayed in the kitchen, supervising what didn't need supervising.

Sunday buffet was the one event during the week she particularly liked to be visible to her customers. Life in small town Texas was several speeds slower than life in Pennsylvania but never more so than on Sunday. She'd learned early on that folks liked to say hi and chat about the weather or their families. The warm, open, and friendly way of the people of Lusty had eased her jitters when she'd first arrived and had, to a large part, contributed to the final stages of her healing.

Up until an hour ago, she would have affirmed that she *had* healed. After all, she'd taken on not one, but two lovers. Wasn't that proof that Kelsey's out of her long blue funk and back to normal?

Now she knew she'd been lying to herself.

She'd gone out to check the supply of food and to meet and greet neighbors, regulars, and new customers.

Her gaze had landed on a little boy.

He's about four.

The same age her Sean had been. His soft brown hair looked in need of combing. That and the serious expression on his face as he set about the business of eating his french fries acted like a giant claw tearing at her heart. Sean had eaten with that singular devotion, and he'd eaten slowly, and nothing she could ever do would hurry him up.

Oh, God. Her eyes flashed to the parents of the little one. Neither of them looked familiar to her.

Her gaze caught the attention of another diner, a man who'd been coming in twice a week for the past few weeks, and she nodded absently to him when he seemed to want her attention.

She turned her gaze back to the young family. The look of sheer, absolute, and total devotion on the face of the little guy's mother twisted that claw around her heart. Her eyes flooded, and she turned, hustled back to the kitchen, then on into the staff washroom.

For long moments, she'd gulped back the tears and the overwhelming grief that at one time had been an ever-present black hole, sucking her in and sucking her deep.

I wish I'd gone into the store with him. Why didn't I go in? I'd wrap my arms around my baby and keep him safe. Or die with him. I should have died with him. Oh God, why didn't you let me die with him?

Kelsey splashed cold water on her face, and after a few long minutes, the grief began to ebb. She sat on the closed toilet, her focus on breathing and on trying to gather those emotions back up and stuff them back in their box.

It had been a very long time since she'd had a grief attack. For the first couple of years after she'd buried her husband and her son, they'd come unpredictably, hard, and often. She never would have thought a body could hold so many tears. Then, as time had passed, the moments came less and less often.

Kelsey blinked as she realized this was the first attack she'd had since moving here to Lusty. The first one in more than six months. That wasn't to say she never thought about her baby. She thought about him at least once, every single day, but, somehow, she'd been able to get through the days, to function, even to laugh.

The best thing to do when the attack hit was to just keep busy. And avoid whatever it was that had triggered it. No, that was something she'd just made up now, but it made perfect sense to her. She'd stay in the kitchen for an hour or so, just until she could be sure that young family had left.

Kelsey knew she was being a coward and was fine with that. So she concentrated on making more salad, cleaning the kitchen, and refilling trays. She focused, worked, and ignored the looks her staff sent her and prayed for that hour to pass.

She didn't know why she looked up when Michelle came into the kitchen. The look of worry on the woman's face made her heart thud and sweat break out all over her body.

"What's wrong?"

"Kelsey, you better come out here. I think we have a problem."

Since Michelle turned and went back into the dining room, Kelsey followed. The woman had stopped and had her attention fixed on a particular table. Kelsey followed her gaze and swallowed hard.

The little boy who looked like her son had fallen asleep in the booster seat.

For a dreadful moment she thought he was dead. Then she saw him twitch, saw a smile come and go, and realized he was dreaming. She exhaled shakily.

"His parents are gone," Michelle said.

Kelsey looked at her, the words not making sense. "What do you mean, gone?"

"I mean, they left. I didn't see when. I'm sorry. I noticed the little guy drift off and the mom stroking his hair. I noticed because she looked kind of sad. Then I got busy, and the next thing I knew, they were gone. I thought at first they'd gotten up to go to the bathroom, and although I wouldn't have left my child alone like that, I could understand how some might, especially if the little guy was sleeping."

"His parents can't be gone. How could they make a mistake like that and leave their baby behind?" No way, that's how. Kelsey had seen that look on the mother's face. She'd felt that look, *lived* that look. There was no way she would have forgotten...

"Oh, my God." Kelsey turned to Michelle, who was nodding because she, Kelsey, had finally gotten it.

The little boy's parents hadn't forgotten him. They'd *abandoned* him.

Kelsey didn't think. She just reached into her pocket and pulled out her cell phone. She punched number three on her speed dial. The phone was answered on the second ring.

"Sheriff Kendall, it's Kelsey Madison over at Lusty Appetites. Could I speak to Matthew, please? It's important."

* * * *

"For a man who's getting regular sex, you're a mite tense there, Deputy Benedict."

Matthew narrowed his eyes, his gaze slicing right through the man who'd spoken those teasing words. His steely-eyed glare might work on most men, but it seemed to have absolutely no effect whatsoever on his cousin Adam. And since his cousin was also his boss, he supposed he could let the comment slide.

Like hell.

"If my mood isn't to your liking, *Sheriff Kendall*, perhaps we could step outside around back and...talk about it." Matthew gave Adam his best smile.

Adam's shit-eating grin just pissed him off even more. "We could do that, *Deputy*, but I'll take you, same as I always do."

"I'm bigger than I used to be," Matthew warned.

"Yeah, but I have a ton of sexual frustration to add fuel to *my* fire. Seriously," he stepped over to the coffee pot, poured two cups, and handed Matthew one, "you and Steven spend every spare minute with Kelsey. I thought the three of you were a done deal. I've been expecting any day now that you would ask me to be your best man."

Matthew accepted the brew and the chance to share confidences. Next to Steven, Adam was his best friend, despite the two years between them.

"Yeah, I'd have thought that by now we'd be a done deal, too."

"So what's the problem?"

"It's taking us longer to cut through Kelsey's defenses than we thought it would. Oh, believe me, on a physical level, we couldn't be happier or better suited. But emotionally? She's still locked up tighter than a girls' school at midterm."

Adam sat in his chair behind his desk and relaxed back. "I guess that's only to be expected. None of us can really understand what she's been through. You just have to be patient with her."

"Oh, I know. We both know. And we're not giving up on her. She doesn't really understand it, but she's ours, and we're keeping her. That part is definitely a done deal." He paused for a moment to sip his coffee. He thought of the way Kelsey had resisted awakening this morning, the way she'd snuggled down between them so sweetly. He especially thought of the way she seemed to totally relax as soon as she arrived at the ranch. "I'm certain she feels more for us than she's willing to admit."

"Getting her to admit it is the problem?"

For the most part, he and his brother thought so. "Yeah. Steven and I have just about run out of ideas. We took Mom's advice and asked Kelsey to help us redecorate the front parlor at the ranch. Mom says that should start sending the message that we're serious and help her to develop a sense of belonging there. If you have any suggestions to add to the mix, we'd be obliged." He got up and paced toward the window. He stood for a long moment, watching people and traffic.

"That's not the heart of it, is it?"

Adam's quiet voice and the question reminded Matthew that his cousin had inherited more than just a love for wearing a badge from that long ago Adam Kendall. He had the family's sixth sense, too.

"She's never talked about it. Not once. I think…I think before she can admit any emotional attachment to us, she has to open up about her loss."

Matthew wondered what Adam would say to that. Then the phone rang. Adam picked it up on the second ring.

"Sheriff's Department," Adam said. "Hi, Kelsey. Sure, he's right here." Adam held out the receiver. The look in his eyes made Matt's heart skip a beat.

"It's your woman. She sounds funny. Like something's wrong."

Chapter 11

The only message Steven got was something had happened at the restaurant, and Kelsey was at the Lusty Clinic.

He literally raced into town and nearly broke down the door entering the building and didn't even care that several gazes immediately snapped to him. He scanned the small crowd gathered, all people he knew, and spotted Kelsey in the midst of them. In three strides, he reached her, his hands going to her shoulders, his gaze anxious as he took in every inch of her.

"You're all right." The relief was enormous, and he closed his eyes for one moment.

"Of course I'm all right."

Only she wasn't. He knew that in a heartbeat. Whatever brought her here hadn't been any physical injury, but she was hurting. Her face looked drawn, and the tone that came out of her sounded so icy it could have cut granite.

"Let me guess," Adam Kendall said. "Auntie Anna called you."

Steven met the man's gaze and nodded. "Yeah." He really should have known better than to allow that jumbled phone call to upset him. They all loved their Auntie Anna. Not another soul in the entire family knew the great-greats the way Auntie Anna Jessop did. Unfortunately, she couldn't be relied upon to deliver a message or get any kind of the practical details of everyday life straight to save her soul.

Steven shook his head and focused again on Kelsey. Because her expression looked so haunted, he gathered her in for one moment, making his hug as comforting as he could, trying not to let his own emotions show. When she relaxed in his arms, when she wrapped hers around him and held him, Steven sighed. He searched but couldn't see Matthew.

Rather than jump to any conclusions, he asked, "Okay, what happened?"

"They just left him," Kelsey said.

She pulled against his hold, and he let her go but he slid his hands down her arms until he had her hands in his. Grateful she threaded her fingers through his, he nodded to let her know she had his full attention.

"He's just a little boy. How could she just leave him? Doesn't she know how precious he is?"

Kelsey's voice shook with emotion, and Steven's heart turned over.

Adam stepped closer and filled in the details, ending with when he and Matthew rushed to the restaurant.

"He wouldn't wake up at first," Kelsey said. "And when he did, I could tell…just looking in his eyes, I could tell something wasn't right with him."

Steven looked over at Adam, who nodded. "Kelsey said she thought the little guy had been drugged. Matt scooped him up and ran like hell for here."

The clinic was only two blocks away from the restaurant.

"Here's the bag." Michelle came into the clinic, carrying what looked to Steven like a backpack. Adam took it and headed down the hall toward the examining rooms.

"Who's on duty today?" Steven asked. Not that it made any difference. He'd known both of the doctors who ran the clinic all of his life.

Shirley, the middle-aged woman, who as receptionist, secretary and accountant for all intents and purposes ran the clinic, looked up at his question.

"Both Doctors Jessop are here today."

"Do you want to sit down?" Steven asked Kelsey. Michelle had remained, and there were a few other people in the waiting area, cousins that Steven guessed had been dining at the restaurant when the drama unfolded. They were there, he knew, not to be nosy, but to be on hand in case they were needed.

"No. I want to go see what's happening. I want to be in there. I just want to—"

Kelsey stopped talking, but she shook like a leaf. Steven understood, or at least he thought he did, where her mind was, where her emotions were. He looked at Shirley, one of the few people who lived in Lusty who had no family connection to Benedicts, Kendalls *or* Jessops.

"I'm taking her back there. Which room?"

Shirley looked as if she might protest, but then she nodded. "Room three."

"Come on, sweetheart." Steven kept his arm around Kelsey as he walked her down the hall to the appropriate room.

"I've never been in here before. It's larger than I expected."

"The town trust pays for it and keeps it up to the highest standards." Steven kept his voice gentle, understanding Kelsey's inane comment came from nerves.

He knocked once on the door to room three, then opened it.

Kelsey left Steven's side, making a bee-line for the little boy who sat on the examining table looking lost and alone. As soon as she reached him, the little guy reached for her.

Smart kid. Steven looked at his brother, who stood with their uncles, Doctor James and Doctor Adam Jessop. Adam Kendall was sorting through the backpack while both doctors had been speaking in low tones to Matthew.

Likely the little boy felt overwhelmed with so many strange men in the room. No wonder he'd reached for Kelsey.

"How is he?" Kelsey asked.

"Here's your culprit." Adam said.

Kelsey had spoken at the same time Adam had. Steven looked at the bottle he was holding. Uncle James took it, read the label, then opened the bottle.

"This would do it. A mild dose of sleep aid, and it looks like there's a half a pill here, which means a half a pill missing. If that's all he ingested, he should be fine. The blood work will be back in just a few hours. Marc's coming in to run the tests."

"So he's all right?" Kelsey asked. The little guy had laid his head on her shoulder and stuck his thumb in his mouth.

Every man in the room heard the emotion in her voice. Steven wondered if she realized that she was slowly swaying, side to side, rocking the child as she stared at the doctors.

"Benjamin is fine. Aren't you, Benjamin?" Dr. James said.

"Benny," Benjamin said around his thumb.

"Benny, then," Dr. James said. He ruffled Benny's hair, but the boy had closed his eyes, seeming content for the moment just to snuggle into Kelsey.

"So now what happens now? To Benny?" Kelsey looked at each of them in turn. Steven felt his heart twist at the look of anxiety on her face.

"He needs to be watched for the next twenty-four hours," Dr. Adam said. "And awakened every so often just to make sure the medication is wearing off."

"But what—"

"I've called your mother, Adam," Dr. James cut Kelsey off and looked at Adam Kendall.

Kelsey focused on Adam. "Why did he call your mother?"

"Mom's the local magistrate," Adam said.

"Oh. Of course. I guess there'll have to be a court order. Children's Services will have to get involved. Yes, of course."

Steven heard the disappointment in Kelsey's voice and wondered if she did, as well. He looked from Matthew to his cousin Adam. Matthew nodded, and Adam seemed to understand exactly what it was he and his brother wanted to happen next because Adam nodded, too.

"I'll go see if she's here yet," Adam said.

"I want my mommy."

"I know, sweetheart." Kelsey continued to rock Benny, whose eyes began to close.

Matthew stepped forward and ran a hand down the little boy's back. "I'm going to do my best to find her for you, Benny, okay?"

"Are you a police man?" Benny asked.

"I'm the deputy sheriff," Matthew said. Then he used his thumb to indicate Steven. "That's my brother. He's a cowboy."

"Really?" That news perked Benny right up. He straightened and took his thumb out of his mouth. "Do you have a horse? Is it here? Can I see it?"

Steven stepped forward. The wide-eyed tot tugged at his heartstrings. He gave him his best smile and kept his voice soft. "I have about twenty horses. Not here, I keep them at my ranch. We'll see what we can do about letting you have a look at them."

"Cool." Then he laid his head back down on Kelsey's shoulder and closed his eyes again. Steven let his gaze meet Kelsey's, and the emotions he saw swirling there lifted his spirits and laid him bare all at the same moment.

* * * *

Kelsey hadn't wanted to get involved, but the moment she'd realized this poor, precious baby had been drugged, she'd been helpless to resist him.

At the moment, Benny lay against her shoulder, his head finding that special place God gave mothers to cradle their sons. The weight of him in her arms as she held him and the warmth of his tiny body stirred more emotions in her than she felt capable of dealing with right now, but she didn't matter.

Only this precious baby boy mattered.

The door to the examining room opened, and Sheriff Kendall stuck his head in. "The magistrate is here," he said.

"Come on, honey," Matthew said. He stood on one side of her, Steven on the other. Both men's gazes had filled with sympathy, and she felt herself shudder.

Only this baby mattered. Kelsey shuddered again as the memories came, fast and furious. She pushed them away ruthlessly and let the men lead her out of the room.

Tall, with beautifully coiffed red hair and mesmerizing green eyes, Samantha Kendall was a striking woman. Kelsey recalled thinking that once before when she and her husbands had come into the restaurant. Kelsey felt her eyes widen when she recalled that Samantha had not two, but *three* husbands. Adam's fathers, she'd learned just a few weeks ago, were triplets.

At the moment, Lusty's magistrate took in the tiny boy Kelsey held, and her eyes softened.

"How is the little man?" she asked, stroking her hand down the boy's back.

How interesting that she's asking me. "The doctors say he'll be fine. They think he was given just a bit of sleeping medication. He needs to be awakened every couple of hours for the rest of the night."

"He seems very comfortable with you," Samantha said.

"I think it's because he was surrounded by so many big men when I went into the room." Kelsey said.

"You're probably right. I have one of my husbands, Preston, tucked away in the admin office here preparing...ah, there he is."

Preston Kendall looked as if he stepped right off the cover of a men's fashion magazine. Though he had to be in his sixties, he didn't look a day over forty.

"Here you go, sweetheart," he said, handing his wife the paperwork. "Three copies, as you requested." Then he bent down to peer at Benny, who had fallen fast asleep. "He's a lovely child."

Kelsey swallowed the urge to say thank you. Benny was *not* her child. In fact, any moment now, Mrs. Kendall was likely going to—

"This form appoints you as temporary guardian for Benjamin," Samantha said. "If you'll sign on the line above your name, then we'll file this on Monday, taking care of the legalities."

"I'm sorry?" Kelsey felt her heart leap. She couldn't have heard what she'd thought she'd heard.

Samantha gave her a matter-of-fact look. "We don't have a Department of Children's Services here in town. *Someone* has to look after him. Besides, with my son and Matthew on the case, they're likely to find Benny's parents soon." The magistrate shrugged. "This is easiest all the way around, don't you agree?"

"We've lots of room out at the ranch," Steven said. "You and Benny can stay there. With your business it'll be easier if we all pitch in. Plus," he lowered his voice and winked, "I've got horses."

Just then, the door to the clinic opened, and Tracy's mother, Heather Jessop, came in. "Where would you like these?" She held two full-to-bursting shopping bags.

"Here, I'll take them," Preston said. "Your Jeep outside, Steven?"

"Yes, Preston, it is. It's not locked."

"Of course not," Preston said.

"There's some pajamas and enough outfits for a few days, and a few toys as well. We'll have some more things gathered for you tomorrow," Heather said to Kelsey.

Kelsey looked down and saw Matthew and then Steven sign as witnesses each of the three pages that Preston Kendall had produced.

"Here, let me have him for a moment," Steven said. "I think I'm the only one of us who hasn't held him yet."

Kelsey watched as Steven deftly plucked the sleeping child from her arms and settled him in against his big chest. She had the same thought now that she had when Matthew had scooped him out of the booster chair in the restaurant and run with him to the clinic.

The Benedict brothers would make good fathers one day.

With her arms empty, Kelsey accepted the pen and papers from Matthew. She didn't let herself think. She just signed her name in the appropriate place on all three pages.

She handed the pen and papers back to Samantha.

Preston came back into the clinic. "Anna and Jackson have brought over a child's car seat. They said it'll just take a few moments for them to install it, then you're good to go."

Samantha smiled. "With all the grandchildren floating around these days, I doubt you'll want for anything for this little man."

"There was a letter in Benny's bag," Adam said quietly. "I'll come over in a while and show it to you."

Matthew put his hand on Kelsey's back. "Do you need to go back to work, sweetheart?"

"No. Tracy will close up for me. Oh, but I have to tell her."

Heather, who was still there, came over and gave Kelsey a hug. "I'll tell her. Michelle will likely help her. Don't you worry about a thing."

"No." Kelsey felt as if she'd been covered in bubble wrap in that she felt a little outside of herself. Everyone was being so kind and generous, and all for a little boy they didn't even know. "No, I won't worry about anything. Well, except Benny." She turned to look at Matthew and Adam. "I hope you find his mother soon. A little boy—" Kelsey had to stop because her throat tightened and her voice caught.

Too close, too close.

She closed her eyes and inhaled deeply, fought for control. And then she continued. "A little boy needs his mother."

"Don't worry, love. We'll find her," Matthew said.

"You go on, the three of you, and get him settled for the night," Adam said. "I'll begin the preliminary investigation. Don't need two of us for that. And then I'll be by, give you an update, and show you the letter."

Kelsey looked over to where the doctors Jessop stood talking to the receptionist and a couple of townspeople. Kelsey couldn't recall if they were Kendalls or Benedicts, and nodded her thanks.

She received a nod and a smile back.

"You want to sit in back with him?" Matthew asked. The men, one of them holding a sleeping Benny, flanked her as they walked out of the clinic.

"Yes, please."

She'd thought they would have to turn this child over to a nameless, faceless social worker, and she'd almost geared up for that. Now as she got into the back of the Jeep and helped Steven fasten the sleeping little guy into the car seat, she tried to come to grips with the sharp, unexpected turn her life had just taken.

For the next little while, at least, she would be taking care of a child. A little boy child, who on first sight, had reminded her so much of her Sean.

Chapter 12

Benny woke up when the Jeep came to a stop at the ranch. Because it was early summer, daylight still reigned at seven-thirty in the evening.

Kelsey unbuckled the child from his safety seat, but she didn't get a chance to lift him into her arms.

He'd looked out the window and crowed with delight. "Horsies!"

Despite the gravity of the situation and the emotions and memories that had been bombarding her, Kelsey smiled. Was there a four-year-old alive who didn't love horses?

"That's right. Horsies."

"Can I go see them? Can I ride one? Please?"

"How about we just go and say hello for tonight?" Steven said. "It's almost the horsies' bed time."

Kelsey found herself nodding when Steven looked at her, one eyebrow raised as if he asked permission.

"Cool!" Benny seemed wide awake as he scrambled to get out of the Jeep.

The little boy had no qualms about putting his small hand in Steven's large one and trooping off to the outdoor corral.

"We have a lot of young ones in the families," Matthew said when she'd stepped out of the vehicle. He stood beside her, his hand on her back as they both watched Benny with Steven. "Quite often, especially during holiday weekends, we're up to our asses in kids here."

Since he said that with a smile she guessed that meant he didn't mind.

Before long, Benny came running back to her, a huge smile on his face. "Tomorrow I get to meet them all!" He stopped when he got to Kelsey, then yawned.

"Are you hungry?" she asked him.

"I'm thirsty," he said.

At home here as much as in her own apartment, Kelsey took Benny's hand and led him into the house to the kitchen.

"Matthew and I will go and make up the bed in the room across the hall from ours," Steven said.

That was the room Kelsey had been going to suggest they use because it was closest to the master bedroom. "Good. I'll take care of the tummy issues."

She lifted Benny onto one of the stools by the center island and opened the fridge. "We have apple juice, orange juice, and milk."

"I like milk!"

He gave her such a wide smile, she felt her breath catch and her heart squeeze. "Milk it is. Would you like some toast with peanut butter, too?" He'd eaten at her restaurant but that had been a few hours ago. Sometimes, little ones ate like birds and sometimes like elephants.

"Peanut butter!"

Kelsey set a slice of bread in the toaster and poured him a glass of milk. In a couple of minutes, the toast popped, and Kelsey got down a saucer and prepared the snack.

She froze when she saw what she'd done. She'd cut the covered toast into eight finger-like pieces. She used to call them soldiers in an effort to encourage her son to eat them.

Here are your soldiers, Sean. Gobble them down!

Like soldiers, Mommy.

Kelsey yanked herself back to the present.

"Here you are, Benny. Toast with peanut butter."

The little boy ate only a couple of pieces before he pushed the plate away.

"I don't want anymore, Kelsey."

"Okay. Let's go see if the men have your bed ready." If she still had him here tomorrow night, she'd bathe him. Right now, she needed to get him into pajamas and into bed. She felt things happening inside her and wanted to get the boy settled. Then she needed to find herself some privacy.

She couldn't go home. Benny was here, and she was responsible for him, so here she'd stay, too. She'd have to find somewhere to be alone in this house. The place was massive. It shouldn't be a problem.

They made a stop in the bathroom for necessary matters and so she could at least wipe his face and hands. A typical boy, he scrunched his face in response to having it wiped. Then she took his hand and led him into his bedroom.

"Good timing," Matthew said. He and Steven had just finished emptying the bags. There were books and toys and clothes as advertised.

The men had the blankets of the double bed pulled back. The little boy looked at it, his eyes wide.

"Big bed," he said.

"It is," Steven agreed.

"If you wake up in the night and need us," Matthew said, pointing, "we'll be right across the hall."

"Okay."

Kelsey grabbed a pair of pajamas and, in short order, had the boy in them. Steven lifted him and spun him through the air while Matthew held the blankets up. One deposited the child onto the mattress, and the other covered him.

Benny giggled, then yawned. He blinked a few times and then focused on Matthew. "You find my mommy tomorrow?"

"I'll do my best, Benny. Right now, I think Mommy wants you to be good and get some sleep."

Benny put his thumb in his mouth and nodded. "Mommy said Kelsey would babysit me."

Kelsey felt her mouth open and closed it quickly. Adam had said there was a letter. Did she somehow know this child and his mother and not realize it?

"Kiss!"

Since Benny looked at her when he said that, she obediently bent over him and gave him a kiss on his forehead. His small arms went around her, and the scent of soap, boy, and peanut butter swamped her. She pulled back from him and felt a wrenching deep inside her.

Oh, God. Oh, God. Not yet. Trying not to show the turmoil within, she brushed his hair gently with her hand. "Sleep well, honey."

"'Night."

Kelsey couldn't hold on another moment. She turned, her legs carrying her out of the room, her vision already blurred by her tears so that she couldn't see where she was going. Frantic, feeling everything inside her beginning to unravel, she nearly ran as she found her way into the master bedroom, then kept walking all the way through it and out onto the balcony.

The spa tub gurgled in the early evening air, the sound of bubbles and birdcalls all seeming so peaceful, so normal.

A tortured groan came from deep inside her from the black hole she'd carried within her for more than five years. Then came another and another. Her knees gave out, and she ended in a squat, her body curving in on itself as she gave herself over to the despair seething within her as she finally broke.

* * * *

Matthew's heart tore apart.

He looked over at Steven, unsurprised to see his brother's eyes, like his own, filled with tears.

Unable to bear it a moment more, he went to Kelsey, lifted her into his arms. She struggled, and he held her tighter.

"It's all right, baby. It's all right."

He brought her over to the bench, moving her so that she lay across his lap and Steven's who sat down beside him.

"It's not all right! It can never be all right! My baby, my baby, my baby!"

Kelsey sobbed uncontrollably, and Matthew had never felt so helpless. He swallowed over the lump in his throat.

"We're so sorry, love, so, very, very sorry." Steven's voice shook with emotion.

Matthew held her tighter, his head resting on hers when her struggles stopped, and she just sobbed. Steven, beside him, stroked her legs. He slipped her shoes off her and rubbed her feet.

Matthew crooned to her, not words so much as sounds, an echoing of her pain, an acceptance of the tears she shed, tears he knew had been buried far too deep for far too long.

Her sobs dwindled to tiny hiccups. She clung to him now, her body purged not only of grief but of strength.

He looked around, needing something, then raised one eyebrow when Adam stepped out onto the balcony carrying a glass of brandy and a box of tissues.

"Boy's asleep," Adam said. "I'll wait downstairs."

Matthew eased Kelsey onto the seat between himself and Steven. His brother, tissues in hand, lifted her face and dabbed at her tears.

"I'm sorry," Kelsey said.

"Don't you ever dare apologize for this." Steven grabbed another tissue, folded it, and held it to her nose. "Blow."

She did, around a laugh that was weak, but a laugh just the same.

Matthew held the glass of brandy to her lips. "Take a sip, baby."

She did, coughing slightly. Matthew patted her back, and Steven rubbed her thigh.

She exhaled, her breath shaky. Her eyes were red-rimmed, her face blotchy, but he'd never seen a more beautiful woman in his entire life.

"I saw Benny with his mother. It must have been an hour before Michelle told me he'd been left." She paused and took another sip of brandy. "He was eating french fries, one at a time, exactly how my Sean used to eat them. And then he looked at his mother and made a face." She stopped, and fresh tears spilled over her eyes, but she didn't sob. Steven mopped her face again and placed a kiss on her nose.

"I turned away from him because the sudden flood of memories hurt so much. I locked myself in the bathroom until I got myself under control. Then I went back to work. Work saved me. Before, too, you know? Keeping busy was all I could do."

"We've never lost anyone," Matthew said. "We can't know what it feels like. But we love you, and your pain is now our pain."

She jerked at that and turned her widened eyes to him and then Steven.

"Sorry, sweetheart," Steven said. "We do love you. Totally and completely. We lied about this being just physical for us."

"Oh." Kelsey looked as if she didn't know what else to say.

Matthew smiled because that one word conveyed volumes.

"And we're not going to let you hide from us emotionally anymore," he said to her. "You're not the kind of woman who can give herself in sexual abandon to anyone she doesn't love, so don't go and try telling us you don't love us. We know you do and have from the start."

"You're kind of macho all of a sudden," Kelsey said. He looked at her face and couldn't read any real anger there. Confusion, yes. And, if he wasn't mistaken, he could see hope in her eyes as well.

"Honey, I'm from Texas. We *invented* macho."

Kelsey shook her head and chuckled just a little. "So I'm beginning to discover."

She sat quietly for a moment, still inhaling shakily.

Matthew reached down and twined his fingers with hers. Steven did the same with the fingers of her right hand.

"We want you to share them with us," Steven said. "Sean and Philip, too. You loved them both, and they're a part of you."

"Can you do that, baby? Can you share them with us?" Matthew asked.

When she met his gaze, he kept his level, hoping she could see the love he held for her shining in his eyes.

She met Steven's gaze as well. He knew they were asking for a greater intimacy than she'd been prepared to give them. To his way of thinking, it was time.

"Yes, all right. I'll…I have a picture album. It's in storage. I'll get it."

"Thank you." Matthew kissed her, keeping the caress light.

Steven turned her face to him and gave her a gentle kiss as well. She responded to them both as she had from the first, sweetly and with unlimited heart.

"Do you want us to ask Adam to come back tomorrow?" Steven asked. "He won't mind."

"No. He's here now. Let's see what he has to say."

* * * *

"I don't understand," Kelsey said just a few minutes later. "Are you telling me she knew me? That she left Benny at my restaurant *on purpose?*"

Adam handed her the note, and she read it, the same words he'd just finished reading aloud to them all. The message, written on plain white paper, the penmanship poor, was short and to the point.

I read about your place in the paper and about how you lost your boy. You have a kind face, and I think you could come to love my Benny. I've got no work, and I can't feed him. And Deke doesn't like him much. I worry sometimes that he'll get mad and start beating him, too. Benny will be safe with you.

"That poor woman." Kelsey looked up, focusing on Adam and then her men.

"We got a pretty good description of her and the man she was with. I dusted the letter for prints and got a partial, and I've sent it off. We have an idea of the make and model of the car they were in, though no plate number, of course."

"No, that would be too easy," Matthew said.

"We questioned Benny last night, but all he told us was his name," Adam said. "Can hardly blame the little guy. He was terrified, still fighting off the drug he'd been given. We'll try again tomorrow. He's only little but he likely knows his last name, at the very least. Anyway, I thought it might help, understanding why his mom thought she had to leave him."

"I'll be in the office first thing in the morning," Matthew told Adam. He turned to look at Kelsey. "You're off tomorrow, and Steven will be here, but we need to think about Tuesday, in case we don't find Benny's mom right away."

"I bet Mom would be happy to come babysit," Steven said.

"That's what I was thinking. Kelsey?"

She couldn't deny they'd have to make some sort of arrangement for the little guy if they still had him on Tuesday. "Maybe she could come for coffee tomorrow," Kelsey said. "Then Benny could meet her."

"Sounds like a plan." Adam got to his feet. "Oh, before I forget..." He left the front parlor and went to the entrance hall. Scooping up a box, he handed it to Kelsey. "Shirley sent that over. It's a baby monitor with three different receivers. She said the instructions are inside the box, along with new batteries."

"Perfect! I'll have to call her and tell her thanks in the morning," Kelsey said.

Matthew and Steven both wore such confused looks, she laughed. "I know he's not a baby, but with this we'll hear him if he wakes up."

While Steven and Matthew walked Adam out, Kelsey made her way upstairs with the monitor. Benny was sound asleep, one of the toys Heather had collected and given them—a blue walrus—clutched tight in his arm, his thumb in his mouth. She set up the monitor, ensured it was working, then left him to his slumber.

In the master bedroom, she set one of the receivers on the dresser and turned it up. She could hear the ticking of the clock on the wall in Benny's room. *Good.*

Alone, the quiet of the evening settling around her, Kelsey walked out onto the balcony. The residual shakes from her crying jag seemed to be gone. Stepping close to the railing, she caught just a slight breeze and inhaled deeply. The air smelled of approaching rain, fresh and clean, as if moisture had already scrubbed the air, making it new again.

In some ways, she felt new again, too.

Kelsey didn't hear a sound, but she knew when Steven and Matthew were standing behind her.

"You said you love me."

She turned then and faced them. To their credit, they stood solemnly and took her scrutiny.

"We did," Matthew said.

"I don't know how I feel about that."

"We know," Steven said. "You don't have to know how you feel about it, Kelsey. Not right now."

"All you have to do," Matthew said, "is let us love you."

Kelsey trembled inside, a different feeling from the one she'd just gotten over. These men reached something in her she'd thought to keep hidden forever. They made her *feel* when she'd convinced herself she was perfectly happy with numbness. She didn't think she was ready for that. She didn't think she really had a choice in the matter.

She'd stayed numb because she'd been afraid. Now, she thought that maybe, just maybe, the brothers Benedict could keep her safe so she wouldn't have to be afraid anymore.

It was, she thought, time to begin emerging from her self-imposed cocoon. "I'm not really sure I know how to do that, either. I'm not sure I know how to let you love me."

Steven and Matthew traded a look. Then they both held out a hand to her. "Let us show you," Steven said.

Kelsey hesitated for one moment. Then she stepped forward and took their hands.

Chapter 13

They led her into the bedroom, to the side of the bed they'd already stripped of blankets. Matthew cupped her face and kissed her, his tongue brushing her bottom lip, then sliding into her mouth. Hot, bold, he tasted her completely, a sipping, sucking kiss that made her feel as if he drank her. He stepped back, stroked a finger down her face, and gave her the most tender smile she'd ever seen. He walked over to the bedside table, took a long match out of the drawer, and struck it.

Steven turned her to him and ran his hands down her arms. "You are so very perfect for us. I'd feared we'd never find you."

Kelsey felt overwhelmed by his declaration. What did they want from her? She opened her mouth to ask that, but Steven gently placed his finger on her lips.

"No. Don't say anything. Just accept what we feel for you, what we give you, however we give it to you, as a gift."

Another macho male. Before the thought could rile her, he slipped his arms around her and laid his mouth on hers.

Instantly carnal, his kiss ignited the embers that seemed to lie banked within her, just waiting for one of these men to set them ablaze.

With slow, lazy strokes, Steven's tongue seduced her. Kelsey felt her muscles weaken and anchored her arms around him. The action brought her closer to his body, and the sensation of his denim-covered erection pressing against her set off tingles in her belly.

Steven broke the kiss gently, then locked his gaze with hers as he began to undo the buttons of her white blouse.

Matthew pressed himself against her back. He'd turned off the lights so that the room, bathed in the glimmer of candles, took on an even more intimate ambience.

"Will you let me take that pretty ass of yours tonight, sweetheart?"

Just the suggestion of anal play made her shiver and burn. Her cunt released moisture, and arousal began its upward spiral, setting every nerve ending in her body ablaze.

"Yes. Anything. Everything." Never had she believed she could feel the heat and desire these men made her feel. Every touch melted her resolve to stay aloof. Every kiss melted her bones, making her feel as if, any moment now, she would become a puddle at their feet.

Steven removed her blouse while Matthew opened her bra. Sliding the lacy garment from her body, Matthew bent and nipped her shoulder, then kissed the small sting away.

Steven petted her from her collar bone to her navel, his work-roughened hands arousing her nipples into hard, eager peaks. Matthew nibbled where her neck met her shoulder, and she let her head fall back where it was cradled on his shoulder, giving him freer access. She felt his fingers at the fastening of her skirt. The garment loosened and then fell.

Steven knelt before her. "Easy." He lifted one foot at a time, pulling her skirt free, tossing it aside.

His hot breath brushed her sopping pussy when he leaned forward to pull her thong panties off her.

"You smell so delicious," he whispered. "Your own particular nectar is the most arousing thing I've ever inhaled."

His words completely stole her strength. She whimpered. As if that was all he'd been waiting for, Matthew scooped her up and laid her on the bed.

"Open for us, baby. Let us look at you. Let us love you." The deep, sexy timber of Steven's voice rumbled in her belly, and Kelsey was helpless to resist him. She didn't want to resist. She just wanted to give and take and bask in the attention these men lavished on her and the sensations they created in her.

She spread her legs wide and watched them devour her with their eyes as they peeled out of their clothes. Steven's chest was broader, more ripped than Matthew's, likely the result of never-ending ranch work. Matthew's muscles appeared more subtle, but she knew from the ease with which he could pick her up that he was as strong as his brother.

Both of their cocks were big, bold, and beautiful.

They came down onto the bed, one on each side of her. Together the men began to touch and kiss, to cup and caress and squeeze, and Kelsey felt a moan of pure delight flutter out from deep in her soul.

"Have you ever seen anything more beautiful than our woman when she's aroused?" Matthew asked.

"Never," Steven said. "Passion looks good on you, Kelsey." He bent down and sucked her right nipple into his mouth. His draw, steady and deep, tugged at her belly and fluttered her pussy.

"That feels so good." When they moved her arms above her head, she relaxed and let them arrange her as they would. Open, vulnerable, she knew with absolute certainty she was safe with them. They could do anything they wanted to her.

I belong to them.

She held the thought close, not willing to put it into words. Then her mind shut down as her body hummed with growing heat.

Matthew nipped her left nipple, then smoothed his tongue over it. Hands caressed her flesh on both sides of her body, working down. They spread her legs wider, then lifted them until they draped male hips. The brush of fingers against the inside of her thighs had her juices flowing even more freely, and the air coming through the open balcony doors kissed her wet folds, adding another dimension to her arousal. She shivered, and her nipples beaded even tighter.

They stroked so close to her clit, but not close enough. Her body chased the touch it craved, her hips lifting from the bed. Soft male chuckles laid down another layer of passion, and Kelsey reveled in the heat, the soaring of her arousal, and the pounding of her heart.

Needing to give as well as take, she brought her arms down so that she could curl her fingers around turgid male cocks. The hot silk over steel responded to her grip, to the squeeze and glide as she moved her hands up and down, caressing them.

The men continued to pet and stroke as if all that existed in the world for them was to touch her and pleasure her. They kept avoiding the tiny bud of her clit, and a groan of frustration emerged from her unbidden.

"Horny, darling?" Steven leaned down to nibble her ear and lick her neck. She turned her head to him, opened her mouth, and sought him.

This kiss was raw, fevered lust. Kelsey sucked his tongue into her mouth, stroking it with her tongue in the same way she would his cock, knowing he'd understand her actions and it would drive him wild.

Steven leaned closer and plunged two fingers inside her.

"*Yes!*" The climax bowed her off the bed, the thrilling ride taking over her body, flinging her up, up, to impossible heights. Electricity shimmered and crackled through her, the sensations so powerful she could barely catch her breath as they consumed her completely.

She came down, and they held her, caressed her. She closed her eyes, and they seemed to want to give her a moment because their touch, more subtle, turned soothing. They moved on either side of her, and then the sound of paper tearing and the roll of latex told her of their intent.

Matthew knelt on the bed, slipped his arms under her, and lifted her. He handed her to Steven who arranged her so that she sprawled atop him. She felt the incredible heat of his sheathed cock against the still quivering, wet folds of her cunt.

"Take me inside you, baby," Steven whispered.

She lifted slightly, then slid, the girth of him spreading her wide, the length of him sliding all the way until it nudged the tiny opening of her cervix. "*Oh, God.*" That nudge of pain acted like a trigger, reawakening her arousal.

"Yeah, ride me, Kelsey."

She did, raising and lowering herself in a rhythm that was at once avid and restrained. She kept her movements slow, enjoying the glide of him within her, the friction against her clit and her G-spot bringing her arousal to new, smoldering heights.

"You feel so good inside me." She braced her hands on his chest to help her move the way she wanted to move. Bending down, she kissed him, her tongue slow and sensuous, her body eager to mate so completely that the imprint of his flavor would stay with her forever.

"Christ, watching you ride my brother's cock turns me on."

Matthew's voice, strained, came from behind her. He reached around her, lifted her hands from Steven, and placed them on the bed.

"Put your head and chest down on him, baby. Stick that lovely ass of yours high for me."

Kelsey obeyed and mewed, the knowledge that soon she would have both her lovers inside her at the same time so thrilling she wondered why she didn't come again just thinking about it.

Steven caressed her hair and then cradled his hand on her head as she rested on his chest. Then Matthew spread the cheeks of her ass. She felt him bend closer and use his tongue to lick her asshole. The darkly intimate action made her mew again.

"I won't hurt you," Matthew whispered, perhaps thinking the sound had been one of feminine distress. She'd taken the largest butt plug they had and worn it for several hours at a time. She loved the feel of it in her, the way it seemed to reach right through her body and tickle her clit from inside. No, Kelsey felt no distress at the prospect of finally taking a cock in her ass, just need—raw, aching need.

"Do it. Oh, please, *do it!*"

"Hold on." Matthew spread some lube on her, and the chill against her hot flesh became a different kind of erotic thrill. She couldn't help but dip her hips and press against his fingers, inviting more.

He worked a finger into her, moved it in a circle, testing her. She felt him add a second finger. Moaning because it felt so damn good, she pushed against his fingers at the same time she pressed down harder onto Steven's cock.

"You're so hot," Matthew groaned. Slowly, he slid his fingers out of her. He moved, changing his position slightly, bringing one foot to lay flat on the bed beside her, and leaned forward. She felt him then, the press of something hot and big against her asshole. He leaned forward, nearly tenting her, and she inhaled deeply as the sting of his invasion bit her and she felt the tiny muscle give way. Burning turned to pain, but the pain increased her desire, pulled her higher than she'd ever been.

Matthew's low growl spoke to her primal woman, the sound evoking hazy images of ancient times, of male dominance and female submission that formed the earliest of human mating rituals.

At that instant, she had no power, no say. Totally at the mercy of the man entering her, the very act of anal penetration demanded she give over completely, trust completely, and take everything.

"Fuck, sweetheart, you are so hot and tight. Just a bit more now."

Kelsey cried out, not in pain, but in amazement as her arousal notched higher and seemed to hold her just on the threshold of orgasm. Matthew clamped his hands on her hips, holding fast. Steven's other hand pressed on her back. She felt his cock, still embedded deep in her pussy, give a slow, forceful pulse.

She squeezed him, and he cursed.

Matthew pressed just a bit harder, shifting the angle of his body, and Kelsey felt him slide the rest of the way into her.

She felt the bounce of his sack on her pussy lips and shivered.

"This is the most incredible thing I've ever felt," Steven said. "I'm surrounded by heat, and Kelsey's cunt just got tighter."

"Move." Kelsey didn't care that she'd been reduced to single syllable utterances. She'd never needed like this. Nothing mattered but that these men move in her, fuck her, make her come.

"Too much, sweetheart? Do you want me out? Just say the word—"

"No. No, don't…just fuck me. Oh, God, please…I need…" Unable to say more, Kelsey pushed back against Matthew, then down onto Steven.

"Easy, sweetheart. I don't want to hurt you. Careful, baby, just let me take it slow…oh, Christ!"

Kelsey's hips surged to fuck their cocks again, her need for more so overwhelming it took her over completely. She didn't want careful or slow. She wanted, needed, hot, hard pounding. She wanted, needed, to be plundered.

Both men swore and Kelsey knew she'd pushed them beyond their control. As if they'd been doing it forever, they all three fell into a rhythm, steamy and fast, hard and deep, back and forth and up and down. The thin coating of civilization dissolved under feral, wanton needs, and Kelsey surrendered utterly, giving over that last little bit of herself she hadn't even realized she'd still clutched close.

Her muscles lax, the tightness in her ass eased. Matthew fucked her, his possession so fierce his balls bounced against her cunt. The sound that emerged from him turned out to be the final push she needed, sweeping her over the edge into a hurricane of rapture, wave after relentless wave of orgasmic bliss battering her, flooding her, consuming her. Steven, too, cried out in completion, and Kelsey could feel the pulsing ejaculations of both of her lovers at the same time.

She came back to herself slowly, the stars that had exploded behind her closed eyelids making her doubt she had vision left while the ringing in her ears suggested she might be deaf. Unable to feel her fingers or toes, she wondered if she was even alive.

"Oh, God." Since that breathy sigh had come from her she guessed she was alive. Matthew had collapsed on her, but his considerable weight felt good.

"Easy, baby," he whispered. "Did I hurt you?"

"No. Good." Maybe in an hour or two she'd become capable of speaking full sentences.

Matthew straightened and then slowly pulled out of her. He lifted her off his brother, gently set her down beside him, then headed to the bathroom.

"Mother of God," Steven said. He wrapped an arm around her and kissed her hair. "I feel like I should erect a statue in gratitude."

"That would certainly give folks something to talk about," she said. As much as she loved lying naked with these two Benedicts, her thoughts traveled across the hall to the little boy sleeping there. She didn't want to shock the little guy should he get up in the middle of the night.

She heard Matthew come back into the room, then felt the bed dip.

"This is Lusty. The only talk you'd hear would be the universal wish that they'd thought of it first. Here, baby."

Kelsey opened her eyes. Matthew had something white in his hands. He seemed to want her to sit up, so she did.

"We'll open the door now. I'll go check on him. Steven will take the next check. Meanwhile, if Benny comes in…" He left the sentence unfinished as he settled one of his T-shirts over her head. She noted that he'd pulled on his boxers. When Steven emerged from the bathroom, he had his on as well.

"Thanks. I was just thinking the same thing."

"It wouldn't surprise me if the poor little guy has a nightmare," Steven said.

"Me, neither," Kelsey agreed. She could easily recall the screams of a child gripped by night terror. It had happened to Sean a couple of times with absolutely no provocation that she knew of. How much more likely, then, that a child abandoned by his mother would have a frightening dream?

Matthew opened the bedroom door and went across the hall just as Steven finished restoring the top sheet and blankets. Matthew returned a few moments later.

"He's fine," he said as he got into bed beside her.

"I love you, Kelsey." Steven placed a kiss on her lips.

"I love you, Kelsey." Matthew turned her head and did the same.

She wished she could say the words back, but something inside told her she wasn't ready. In her world, love equaled commitment, and she just couldn't yet. She might never be able to, but maybe the time had come to leave the past completely in the past and think about the future.

Kelsey nodded off to sleep, her last thought that she might not get to sleep through the night with a wee one in the house.

Later, much later, a scream of terror and torment awoke them all, but the scream wasn't Benny's.

It was Kelsey's.

Chapter 14

"Benny's gone back to sleep," Matthew said as he re-entered the bedroom. He handed the glass of brandy he'd brought to Steven, who held it to Kelsey's lips.

"Sip."

"Thanks." She took a tiny drink, then shivered. "Brandy twice in one night. A new record for me."

"You lush," Matthew said.

Kelsey managed a small laugh. She inhaled deeply and closed her eyes and let herself lean against Steven.

Matthew got back under the blankets, pressing close to her, and stroking her arm. "Can you tell us about your nightmare, sweetheart?"

"It was the shooting," Kelsey said. "For the first year after that horrible day, I'd have the dream on a regular basis. I saw it happen, you see. And then, in my nightmares, it would happen again and again, only I knew it was going to happen. Usually, I'd push myself out of the car, run towards the store, nearly, so very *nearly* making it. Failing, time and again, to save them. To save my baby."

Kelsey felt the tears tracking down her face. Matthew wiped them this time. He said, "You know there's nothing you could have done, don't you?"

"I know. But I'm a mother. I *was* a mother," she corrected. "A mother's first, most sacred duty is to keep her child safe *no matter what*. I didn't keep my child safe. I used to go over it, in my mind, over and over. Philip stopping at the store because he wanted to buy a pack of cigarettes. Sean begging Daddy to go into the store with him because his daddy would almost always buy him a piece of candy. I kept thinking, what if I'd only nagged Philip more to quit smoking? What if I'd spoken up so that Sean wouldn't expect candy every time he went into the store with Daddy? What if..." Kelsey paused, took a deep breath. "Just, what if."

"Sweetheart." Matthew sighed.

"How could you have known what would happen one day? You couldn't," Steven said. "You can just do what seems right, and kind, at the time, can't you? None of this was your fault."

"Oh, I know. I know it's not my fault. That's not always how it feels." She lay back against the stacked up pillows. Her mind replayed the dream that had catapulted her from sleep. Then she frowned. "This one was different."

"How so?" Matthew asked.

"It *felt* different. Usually, I'm in the car, looking at the store, watching Philip's progress through the aisles. He was a tall man. Six and a half feet. When he went into that store carrying Sean, they were always in sight. And I would always watch because sometimes Sean would make the cutest faces. Anyway, the dream always is the same and I have this sense of danger as I'm looking at them. Only, this time, I sensed danger lurking *outside* of the store."

"Maybe because the gunman was about to go in?" Steven asked.

"I...I don't think so," Kelsey said. "Something outside of the store, in the parking lot. Something that made me shiver. And this time, in my dream, when I turned to look back *at* the store, I couldn't see them. I couldn't see Philip and Sean."

"Maybe it was different because you're different," Matthew offered. "Maybe because you're moving on with your life, a little."

"Maybe," Kelsey said.

"Think you can go back to sleep now, sweetheart?" Matthew asked.

Kelsey knew she was still a little shaky from the nightmare. Yet she also felt better in its aftermath than she'd ever felt after one. She snuggled down into the bed and sighed when Matthew and Steven surrounded her with their heat and, yes, their love.

Kelsey's mind lingered on the meaning of her nightmare even as sleep began to claim her again. Maybe Matthew was right. Perhaps the significance of the dream was simple. Maybe her subconscious was telling her that Philip and Sean really were gone, and it was time for her to move on with her life.

* * * *

Matthew found himself easily distracted as he pursued the threads of the investigation the next morning. He and Adam were both deep into the search for Benny's mother. Despite the sense of mission he felt, more than once he found himself stopping and staring off into space.

He'd risen with Steven, showered, and left while Kelsey was still asleep in their bed. Neither of them had wanted to wake her. Steven planned to do just the necessary first-thing-in-the-morning chores, and then, if Benny was still asleep, head back to bed and some private loving time with their woman.

Matthew scanned the data he'd gotten from the Department of Motor Vehicles while his mind also grappled with another mystery. Something about Kelsey's dream nagged at him, but damned if he could put his finger on what or why. Finally, he got up to pour himself a second cup of coffee, then stopped by Adam's desk. He wanted to pull a string. Because it would be a personal use of department resources, he'd run it by Adam. He wouldn't do so if the sheriff said no.

"What's up?" Adam asked.

"I want to call Carmichael over in Austin and ask him to send me the file on the murder of Kelsey's family."

"She was pretty upset last night," Adam said. "It must be hard, trying to take care of your woman without knowing all the facts. Sure, go ahead."

"Thanks." Matthew hesitated for just a moment, then shrugged. "It isn't that. Or rather, it isn't just that. She had a nightmare last night, and when she told me about it, something got my cop instincts quivering."

Adam raised his right eyebrow. "In that case, *hell yes*, go ahead and get that information."

"Thanks." Matthew went back to his desk and put in a quick call to his acquaintance on the Austin P. D. Patrick Carmichael promised to dig the file out of the archives and send it along. He thought it had been stored digitally, which would mean Matthew could have the information as soon as that afternoon, if he was lucky. He thanked the man, then went back to work on the dozens of tiny details that most people didn't realize comprised the brunt of police work.

He and Adam were scanning a list of vehicle registrations. There'd been so many they'd split the list in half.

"Trying to see how many cream and rust-colored ten-year-old Ford Crown Vics there are in this part of the state is proving to be a pain in the ass," Adam said. He sat back, rubbed his eyes. "I was thinking of sending a BOLO to the Highway Patrol, anyway."

"It can't hurt. What about the hospitals?" Matthew asked. He waited and knew when Adam understood.

"Now there's a thought. Woman's scared enough of her boyfriend to leave her child behind, you have to figure the prick's put her in the hospital at least once already."

"I know that article on the restaurant in the Waco *Tribune-Herald* was picked up by papers in Austin and Dallas, but I'm going to focus on the hospitals in Waco. I don't think the woman came from that far away."

"Good thinking," Adam said.

Matthew shrugged. "Hell, I have to do something. I promised Benny I'd try and find his mom today."

"You know," Adam said, "he doesn't seem as upset as I would expect a child to be who'd been dumped with strangers."

"He said something last night about his mother telling him that Kelsey would babysit him. Which means she prepared him for this. Even so, you'd think he'd be hysterical. He is only four. At that age, usually, a kid can't reason well."

"Unless he's had to grow up pretty fast," Adam said.

Matthew nodded. Adam's tone of resignation matched his own feelings. Then he remembered what Kelsey had said in the aftermath of her nightmare last night. "A mother's first sacred duty is to protect her child no matter what," he said now.

"Pardon?"

"After Kelsey's nightmare last night, Steven and I were trying to reassure her that her son's death wasn't her fault."

"Of course it wasn't," Adam said.

"Well, Kelsey said she knew that, but that it had been her duty as his mother to protect her son. Yesterday, I was pretty pissed at the woman who'd desert a little boy, leaving him with strangers. Now I think I'm feeling a little more compassionate. Maybe the woman believed this was her only option to keep Benny safe, to protect her child."

Matthew saw Adam's jaw tighten. His cousin, for all that he was a man of the twenty-first century, had a lot of old-fashioned notions and could be pretty rigid in his beliefs sometimes. In some areas, there was only black and white for Adam Kendall, no shades of grey.

Finally, Adam said, "It's not my place to judge the woman. Let's find her first. You could be right in your assessment, but I'll tell you what I know. Hell, what we both know, really. If she did leave the boy here to keep him safe or to please that bastard she's with—well, that doesn't bode well for her to my way of thinking. She's still likely to get beat on."

"We're certainly on the same page there," Matthew said.

* * * *

"Fucking kid." Connors had been stewing since the evening before, when he'd watched his well thought-out plan disintegrate before his very eyes. Now, twelve hours later, he paced his motel room on the outskirts of Waco and tried to come up with a new plan.

He had to act soon because he was running out of time. He'd had everything planned last night, knew exactly what he was going to do. After making eye contact with that bitch in her restaurant, he was going to "accidentally" run into her as she locked up the place that night. That was one of the few times she was alone, without either one of those muscle-boys hanging around her. He'd watched her lock up several times now, and he knew her routine and the routine of the community. That hick town all but rolled up the sidewalks at night. There would have been no one around to even see him.

Thank God Cora Lynn's mother had fallen and broken her hip. He couldn't believe his luck and had insisted his wife go and stay with her mother in Houston for however long it took for her to be better.

Win-win for him because his wife thought him a hero and he had time to deal with the Madison woman.

He figured he'd been home, and home free, by now.

Desperate times called for desperate measures.

Drawing back the curtain, he peered out at the early morning activity. Folks were traveling, some on vacations, some off to work. Offices and coffee shops and malls would be collecting their employees, getting ready for the retail crowd.

Bleary-eyed, most folks just went about their business, their Monday morning routine so ingrained they never thought twice, never *looked* twice.

An idea occurred to him, and he sat for a moment, thinking it through.

He knew where the Madison woman lived, a small apartment building at one edge of town. He knew where she spent most nights and that she drove herself there. And he also knew that she would return to her own apartment when her lover, whichever one of those pretty boys she was fucking, went to work.

The restaurant was closed today. So she'd likely spend the day doing her errands. She'd be out and about in her car. Yeah, this could work.

He couldn't use his own car, of course. So far, he'd been noticeable but didn't stand out. What he was about to do would sure as hell stand out. Broad daylight. But if he used another vehicle, it would work.

He knew just where he could get that other vehicle, too. He'd have to hustle. No time for a shower and breakfast. He'd grab a coffee and donut at the coffee shop next door and be on his way.

Connors threw his few possessions into his duffle and vacated the room. Within ten minutes, he was approaching the mall he'd passed by each time he headed to Lusty.

A quick check of his watch told him the stores weren't open yet. He pulled his car into a spot some distance from the entrance and proceeded to drink his coffee and eat his donut while he watched the mall's employees arrive for work. Anyone noticing him would figure he was just scarfing down his breakfast before heading inside.

He met his own gaze in the mirror and checked that his disguise held out. He was going to be very glad when he could ditch the padding, wig, and mustache for good.

Returning his attention to the arrival of the employees or, more specifically, their vehicles, he finished his coffee. He picked, then discarded, a few candidates for what he had in mind.

Then he saw it, the perfect car. An older economy model, the vehicle wouldn't possess any of the modern anti-theft devices so popular these days. The driver, a young woman, locked the vehicle by pressing down the inside button instead of with a fob. The car, a shit-brown Taurus, would be perfect. Not only would it *not* stand out, it was larger than the little hybrid the Madison woman drove.

Connors waited a bit longer until the flow of people and cars had eased. Inhaling deeply, he prepared himself to move. He'd gathered a few supplies, just in case. Grateful now that he had, he donned the latex gloves, then touched the lock pick he'd secreted in his pocket. His nerves steady, he set out.

Though he hadn't actually done this for a few years, Wesley found he hadn't lost his touch. He was inside the car in mere seconds. The vehicle was neat and clean inside. That spoke to the personality of its owner. As he'd predicted, no after-market security devices had been installed on this car.

God bless women and their simple little minds and trusting little souls.

The engine started on the first try. He grinned when he saw the car had a full tank of gas. Whistling to himself, he put the vehicle in gear, passed his own parked car, and headed back toward Lusty.

Chapter 15

Kelsey surfaced from a deep well of sleep to the sensation of a hard, naked cock pressed against her bare ass.

She smiled slowly, inhaled deeply, and recognized the scent of her lover. "Steven," she said.

"Good morning, love." He pressed his entire body close to her. His heat penetrated her skin, sinking into her very soul. Arousal and comfort intertwined, filled her, and she sighed in pleasure.

"What time is it?" She kept her voice to a whisper, not wanting words to overwhelm the sensations coursing through her.

"Early yet, not even eight."

"Benny?"

"Still sound asleep. It was late when he finally settled down for the last time last night. I know kids need routines and all, but I vote we let him sleep for a while longer."

"Oh yeah? How much longer would you suggest?" She couldn't keep the seductively teasing tone out of her voice. Steven had begun to rub his cock against her. Her pussy was sopping wet, ready for him.

"Long enough."

She felt his movements against her back. That, combined with the sound of foil tearing, told her what he was doing. Anticipation raced through her blood.

Steven leaned over her, moved her right leg forward, and worked his latex-covered cock between her thighs until he stroked the wet folds of her pussy.

"I was going to play with you until you were ready, but seems like I don't have to."

"Play with me anyway."

His deep chuckle reverberated low in her belly, sending delicious tingles throughout her body. When he caressed her hair then took hold of it, pulling her head back, she tilted her neck for him. His lips, hot and hungry, fastened onto hers.

She opened to him, her tongue sliding and stroking his. He tasted of man and coffee, and the scent of the outdoors clung to him.

"You've been up and out," Kelsey said.

"And here I am, up again."

Kelsey laughed, the laughter turning to a moan of pleasure when Steven moved, sliding his cock all the way into her in one solid thrust.

"You feel so good around my cock, honey." Steven's words tickled her ear. "I love fucking you."

Kelsey never would have believed how incredibly hot it made her to have a lover talk dirty. Now, emboldened by his words and her arousal, she said, "I love having you fuck me."

"Mmm. Did you like having both our cocks in you last night?"

"God, yes." She had never felt so full or come so hard.

Steven moved, taking her with him so that she knelt on the bed, her ass high in the air while he continued to fuck her from behind.

The sensation of his cock moving in and out of her, the friction, the fullness, set every one of her nerve endings on fire. She became so wet, making the glide of the latex-covered girth within her smooth and slick. She felt tingles gathering low in her belly, spreading out, and she groaned. Higher and higher, these fiery spasms swirled within her.

Steven changed his angle, seeming to stretch to the side, and *oh, yes,* his cock began to hit harder and deeper inside her. The twinges of pain rolled into the heat, and Kelsey gasped at the even greater stimulation.

She heard a sound just before she felt the cold slide of lube on her anus. Steven rubbed a finger back and forth across it, then pushed, sinking into her back entrance. He added a second finger and began to finger-fuck her ass in a fast and furious rhythm.

"Oh, God!" Kelsey came in an explosion of orgasmic bliss, the climax flashing through her entire body, consuming her, burning her so that all she could do was cry out in ecstasy and let it take her. She heard Steven's low curse, his muffled shout, and felt the cock in her cunt convulse as he found his own release. Still, wave after wave of pleasure washed over her, and it felt like forever before the climax finally ebbed.

Her hips slid down on the bed until she was lying flat, Steven still on her, in her, as they both fought for breath. She shivered, aftershocks of her personal earthquake shimmering through her, and she wondered how she could actually live through such powerful convulsions.

"Are you all right, sweetheart?"

"Dead."

Steven chuckled. He moved, kissed her where her neck joined her shoulder, then fell to the bed beside her.

"No, you're not. I didn't hurt you?"

"No. It was fabulous."

He gathered her in, and she took a moment to revel in the afterglow and the snuggling. Turning around to face him, she stretched up and laid her lips on his. Easy, comfortable, this kiss conveyed an emotion Kelsey thought was very close to love.

From the dresser, a sound intruded, and Kelsey sighed. "Benny."

"I'll get him. You shower and meet us down stairs. Okay?"

Kelsey smiled. "I won't be long. I'll make breakfast."

"That's a deal."

* * * *

Ginny Rose wiped the dried tears from her eyes as she struggled to awaken. Her gaze took in her surroundings, recognizing a motel room. Beside her on the bed, the sound of snoring sent a shaft of revulsion through her.

She didn't turn her head to look at Deke, didn't think the sight of him first thing in the morning would do anything good for her stomach, which was churning with nausea and bile.

The ache in her right shoulder nearly made her cry out loud, but she was good at hiding her reactions. She reached up with her left hand and massaged the ache.

At least Benny was safe.

She hated herself, hated the life she'd let herself fall into, hated herself for giving in to Deke's pursuit of her. How was she to have known he'd abuse her? He'd seemed so loving and attentive at first. He'd even seemed to like Benny. She'd believed she'd finally done something right, chosen a man who would *be* a man and take care of her and her baby.

But it had all gone to hell. She'd taken the first slaps because he'd continued to be kind to her son, and Benny's well-being was everything to her. When he'd begun to show less patience, when he'd been mean and punishing of the innocent little boy, she'd known she had to do something.

Then had come that horrible ultimatum, a threat uttered one night when Benny had been crying and Deke had been drunk. He'd told her to shut her baby up or he'd shut him up permanently. Ginny knew she needed to do something immediately, something drastic. He'd apologized when he'd been sober, but Ginny no longer trusted his apologies. More than anything she'd wanted to run away, her baby tucked safe to her bosom, but she knew the reality was she couldn't. Deke hadn't finished with her yet. There could be no escape for her. He'd told her he'd kill her if she left him. But if she could make sure that Benny was safe first, then that would be another matter.

She'd recalled reading that article in the paper about the woman who'd opened that restaurant in Lusty. Hell of a name for a town. So she'd convinced Deke that getting rid of Benny was what she wanted to do so they could party more, and she could give him all of her attention. Asshole never looked at her really, so he never saw the way just saying those words, just pretending, tore the very heart out of her.

Ginny hoped with all her heart that, someday, Benny would understand. She knew that even if that woman, Kelsey Madison, didn't step in and take care of her boy, he would be safe.

She pushed away her own memories of growing up in foster care. The authorities were more careful these days, more rigorous in rooting out the pedophiles, giving more care to the children's safety than they had when she'd been in the system.

Ginny inhaled deeply and looked toward Deke, who continued to snore in the bed next to her. She moved as carefully as possible, wincing when the chain of the handcuff that held her fast to the headboard clanged.

There, on the bedside table beside the two empty Jack bottles, lay the key to the cuffs. She had to pee so badly she decided to risk waking Deke by reaching beyond him.

Moving carefully, she inched her way up on the bed, pulling her legs closer to her chest, sidling until she could get her knees under her. Fire shot through her shoulder.

If I could only reach the key.

Deke had locked her up while he'd been so drunk he could barely see. She could only be grateful he'd left the key where she could see it. Reaching it would be another matter.

Kneeling on the bed, she stretched her entire body toward the nightstand, her arm extended, fingers stretched. One eye fearfully watched Deke for any sign that he was awakening. It had been very late when he'd finally passed out, so he likely wouldn't wake up for a couple of hours yet.

Best be careful. No sense tempting fate.

Ginny stretched for all she was worth and bit back the pain and frustration when she saw her reach was just inches short.

Damn it.

She edged her knee closer to the headboard and heard another soft clink of metal on metal.

Looking down, she recognized Deke's belt, nearly off the head of the bed, between the mattress and the headboard, where he'd abandoned it after…

Ginny swallowed hard, the sight of the leather sending chills through her and curdling her stomach. It took everything in her to reach out, take hold of the thing, and bring it closer. Working quickly and one-handed, she folded the stiff leather in half. Grasping one end of the shortened accessory, she reached out, lifting it over Deke's snoring head toward the nightstand. She knew one moment of a strong urge to use the thing on him, on his face, to see how he liked it. She tamped down that impulse because that action would surely get her killed.

Ginny was swept by the sudden and certain knowledge that she didn't want to die. She wanted more than anything to get away from this bastard, find her son, and hold him close.

Stretching, the belt touched the table just beyond the key. Closing her eyes, gathering her strength and, praying, she pulled the belt toward herself quickly.

Thank God. The key hit the mattress, and Ginny set the belt down and picked up the key.

Working quietly, she unlocked the cuffs. Easing from the bed, she inhaled deeply as she gained her feet and blinked back tears. She hurt in so many places, but the deepest wound was one that had no bruise or abrasion. The deepest wound was in her heart.

My baby.

She used the facilities quickly, then ran the water just lightly enough to be able to wash her hands and face. She gave herself a quick look in the mirror, wincing at the sight of the bruise on the side of her face. She didn't check the rest of her body. She didn't want to see the welts. She could feel them. That was enough.

Leaving the tiny haven, she let her eyes roam the nondescript room. She had no luggage here. She hadn't known Deke had planned to stop at a motel, or that instead of returning home to Waco, he'd decided to head to Abilene to visit a friend of his.

The words he'd said before getting completely drunk last night brought a chill to her now.

Moose is my best buddy, and he knows how to handle a woman. You'll see.

Ginny didn't know how far they'd driven after leaving Benny. She didn't really know where she was. She *did* know she couldn't stay another day with Deke. Benny was safe, so she could try and escape now.

She grabbed her clothes, dressed quickly. Next, she gathered her shoes and her purse and searched for Deke's wallet. Finding it, she opened it and scanned the sparse contents. Helping herself to the fifty there, she tossed the wallet back down, then headed for the door. Easing it open, she slipped outside, pulling the door gently shut behind her.

She knew enough to know they'd been heading north after they'd left Benny. If she wanted to go back to her son, she needed to head south. Taking only a moment to put on her shoes, she gave a glance at the car before turning and walking toward the end of the building.

Looking around, she fixed her bearings and began to walk. Nerves told her to run, and so she did. The motel had been on a country road at the bottom of an exit ramp from the highway. She ignored the roads and instead struck out across country. It would be harder walking, but Deke would never be able to follow her where he couldn't drive.

Frightened, yet determined, Ginny began to run for her life.

* * * *

Kelsey really liked Bernice Benedict. She hadn't been certain how she would feel sitting face-to-face with the older woman over the kitchen island now that she was sleeping with two of Bernice's sons. Any fears she might have had about the older woman harboring any animosity toward her vanished within the first few moments of her visit.

"So here's the little man who's captured the heart of Lusty." Bernice's greeting had made Kelsey smile. It was true. Benny had captured the heart of the entire town. A delivery of clothing and toys had come just after breakfast, and that act had been repeated over and over again ever since.

Kelsey brewed a fresh pot of coffee, then sat across from Bernice as they both watched Benny playing on the floor with his some of his new toy trucks.

"Any word yet from Matthew?" Bernice asked quietly.

"Just that he hasn't found her yet," Kelsey responded softly. "That poor woman. Imagine feeling so desperate…"

Bernice shook her head. "I can't. It's simply beyond my experience. There's never been a problem, or an obstacle, that either me or one of my husbands hasn't been able to surmount. Even during the hardest times, there's always been a slew of family—Benedicts, Jessops, Kendalls, and Parks—to lend a hand."

Kelsey tilted her head to one side as she considered the woman and the statement she'd just made.

She opened her mouth to ask a question, then thought better of it. Bernice, however, proved that she was at least as observant as her sons. Reaching forward, she laid a hand on Kelsey's and squeezed.

"It's not always easy balancing two men, but in my experience, it certainly is worth it."

Kelsey sighed. "It still seems surreal to me. As though, I don't know…"

"As though someone is going to come out of the woodwork at any moment and condemn you for daring to follow your heart?"

"Yes." Although Kelsey hadn't said the words to the men the way they had said them to her, she felt love for them within her. Making love with both of them at the same time *was* following her heart.

"I have to admit that I felt that way at first myself. Outside family can be a deterrent, too. My father never came to accept my lifestyle, although my mother did." Bernice shrugged. "What I do know is that both Jon and Caleb were meant for me, and I for them. They each meet separate needs in me." Then she leaned forward. "One day, when you come visit us at the big house, I'll show you Sarah Carmichael Benedict's journal. She wrote it not long after her sons courted and then married Madeline Kennedy. I guess in helping her daughter-in-law to adjust to the reality of loving two men, she figured her words and insights could help future generations. By then, their dream, a town where people could live and love as they chose, had become a reality."

"I'd like that." Mention of the journal brought to mind the promise she had made Matthew and Steven the night before about a different sort of journal.

Steven came into the kitchen just then, kissed his mother and her, and then looked down at Benny.

"Does anybody here want to go see some horses?" he asked the room in general.

"I do! I do!" Benny jumped up and down in excitement.

Bernice announced she wanted to go out to the barn, too. "It's been too long since I've come out to the ranch to visit."

"This would be a good time for me to go and get those photo albums," Kelsey said. She felt no qualms leaving Benny in the hands of the Benedicts. Steven was so good with the little guy, and Benny and Bernice had taken to each other on sight. "I have them in a storage locker off the highway between here and Waco."

"McCluskey's?" Steven asked.

"Yeah. I put a lot of my stuff in storage there when I moved from Austin. I should be back in an hour or so," Kelsey said.

"Take your time, love. We're going to be busy in the barn."

Ten minutes later, Kelsey waved as she navigated the car out of the driveway and headed toward Lusty. Because she was driving farther than just her usual five minute jaunt between the ranch and the restaurant, she'd activated her Bluetooth and set her cell phone in the console beside her. Traffic was never brisk through town, especially in the morning. She turned the radio on low and took her time driving through the small town. Looking around, Kelsey shook her head. Even today, she could see families, groups of people who lived and loved together, standing in front of stores where they'd obviously bumped into friends coming and going. Yet she'd never noticed until Matthew and Steven had taken her to the museum and out to the ranch that first time that a happy couple more often than not included three or even four people.

"Talk about being blind," she said aloud as she stopped at the only traffic light in town. It turned green, and she passed the museum and then the sheriff's office. Matthew and Adam's cars were both there, and she lifted a hand in a wave, not knowing if anyone saw her or not. Soon she was motoring past her apartment building on her way towards the state road and her destination.

I should stop on the way back and grab some more clothes for myself.

She needed to do laundry but could do it at the ranch.

She accelerated once she reached the state highway, and her cell phone rang. Reaching up to her Bluetooth, she pressed the button.

"Hello?"

Matthew's smooth voice came over the line. "Hey, pretty lady." Kelsey smiled because she could hear the smile in his voice. "Where you headed on such a fine morning?"

"Out to the storage place to get those photo albums. How's it going?"

"Slowly. When I saw you drive past, I decided I needed a break. I'm only about a minute behind you."

Before she could say anything, her car jolted, and she gasped.

"What's wrong?" Matthew's voice left teasing behind.

"Some son-of-a-bitch just rammed—" She was jolted again, harder this time. Her eyes flicked to the review mirror. A Ford Taurus had pulled back but began accelerating again. "Fuck off!"

"Kelsey!"

"Asshole in a tan Taurus seems to be…Oh, shit, he's coming up beside me. Matthew!"

He was yelling in her ear, but Kelsey couldn't answer. It took all her concentration to hang on to the steering wheel. The Taurus rammed her car on the driver's side, and she spared a glance but didn't recognize the hat-wearing driver behind the wheel. Uncertain whether to speed up or slow down, she began to apply the brake.

Was the asshole drunk? Kelsey spared him another glance. He seemed to be widening the gap between them. Then he narrowed it again. This time, the impact was harder, and Kelsey lost control of the car. It left the road and careened toward a tree.

She had no time for more than a sharp curse as car met tree and glass shattered and metal screamed.

Chapter 16

The moment Kelsey gasped and told him she'd been rammed, Matthew turned on his lights and siren and stomped on the gas. Then she swore, and he heard the sound of the other car ramming her, and his heart tripped in his chest as he screamed Kelsey's name.

He knew he couldn't be more than thirty seconds behind her. He crested a small hill and saw in heart-stopping clarity what he heard with sickening dread through the cell phone. Kelsey's car hit a tree.

The Taurus that had run her off the road had come to a stop but now sped off, likely in response to Matthew's siren. The driver swerved in his haste to pick up speed. Matthew caught the first three letters of the license plate, saying them over and over to himself so he wouldn't forget.

He very badly wanted to wrap his hands around that bastard's neck and squeeze the living shit right out of him, but he had to let him go.

Police procedure dictated in this kind of situation that the victim came first.

"Oh, Christ." He couldn't think of Kelsey as a *victim*. Bringing the cruiser to a screeching halt, he jammed the gearshift into park and practically leapt from the vehicle. Running for all he was worth, he reached her car, yanking and yanking until he got the driver's door open, calling her name the entire time.

Kelsey moaned in pain, and it was the sweetest sound he'd ever heard. Bits of plastic littered the interior of the car, and his woman, still strapped in, sat with her head back against the seat.

"Sweetheart?" His hands shook as he stroked her. He took a moment to examine her and the car. He'd move her if he had to but wanted to see how badly she was hurt first. There was no smoke coming from under the hood and no smell of gasoline. So far, so good.

"Oh, fuck."

"My sentiments exactly." As he watched, she opened her eyes, blinked, then turned looked at him.

"Hi."

"Hi yourself. I want to get you out of here. Where does it hurt?" He couldn't keep his hands off her. She was alive. She could talk.

He'd been a cop long enough to know she could easily have been killed.

"I think I bumped my head."

"Yeah, I see a bit of a goose egg coming up. Anything else?"

"Shoulder where the seat belt grabbed me. I wasn't going very fast, Matthew. As soon as that jackass pulled up beside me, I slowed down. I guess I should have stopped. I never expected him to ram his car into the side of mine like that."

"Most people can't think rationally in a moment like that, baby. Thank God we were talking at the time. Okay, I'm calling for an ambulance."

"I don't need an ambulance. Really. They'd just cart me off to Waco, and I'd be in the ER for hours. "

"You're fucking getting an ambulance. Deal with it."

He just stared at her as she unfastened her seat belt. Because she seemed determined to get out of the car, he helped her. He kept his hands on her until he saw she was steady.

"See? I'm standing on my own two feet. I'm shaking, a bit sore, a little scared, and a lot pissed off. But I'm not hurt badly. I don't need an ambulance."

She was standing *and* lucid. "Fine, then you're going to the clinic in Lusty. Come sit in my car while I call Adam."

"Can we go to the storage place first, since we're almost there? I want—"

Matthew stopped and stepped in front of her, and she must have finally realized how coldly furious he was because she immediately shut up then shrugged her shoulder.

The shrug made her wince.

"We are going immediately to the clinic. If you say one more word about going anywhere *but* the clinic, it'll be the hospital in Waco for you. Nothing, absolutely nothing, is more important to me at this moment than making sure you're okay. Got it?"

"Got it."

He drew her into his arms and held her. He knew she could feel that he was shaking. He didn't care. "Scared the living hell right out of me. I thought we'd lost you."

He felt her arms come around him, and he felt *her* trembling. "I thought you'd lost me, too."

He led her to his cruiser, then eased her into the front passenger seat. He took a moment to run back to her damaged vehicle. Her purse had tumbled onto the floor, and he grabbed it, making sure he got everything that had fallen out of it. He returned to his own car and called Adam. He told him what had happened and gave him the information he had on the Taurus. Then he shut the radio off and turned the car toward home.

"Adam's contacting the highway patrol. They'll likely meet him at your car. Adam's already issuing a BOLO. Once they've finished forensics, it'll be towed. Gord Jessop has one of the best car repair shops in the entire county. They'll probably take it there."

"Okay. The guy must have been drunk."

Matthew divided his attention between the road and his woman. "Don't close your eyes, baby. I don't want you passing out on me."

Kelsey laid her head back. "I don't feel anywhere near to passing out. I've got a mild headache, is all."

"I've no doubt. You're also likely black and blue all over." And if she wasn't really sore right now, she would be in the morning. It only took about twenty minutes to drive back to Lusty. Matthew pulled his cruiser to the curb in front of the clinic. He wasn't surprised when Steven's Jeep squealed to a stop right behind him. Steven had the passenger door of the cruiser open and was lifting Kelsey out of the car before Matthew rounded the hood.

"Jesus." Steven's face looked white and tight with fear.

"I'm all right, Steven. Where's—"

"Mom's at the ranch with Benny. Adam called me."

Kelsey didn't argue about being carried. Matthew followed his brother and Kelsey into the clinic. Shirley had the door open to the first exam room, and Doctor James Jessop was already there, waiting for them.

"All right, let's have a look at what you've done to yourself. Gentlemen? If you would give us some privacy?"

Matthew looked over at his brother, then turned back to his Uncle. "She's ours," he said. "We're not going anywhere."

* * * *

Kelsey had never been fussed over like this.

At first she'd wondered whose idea it had been to keep her so occupied with visitors she didn't have a moment to think about the accident. Then she realized that, much as the people of Lusty had immediately pitched in to provide for Benny, they'd jumped at the chance to pamper her, too.

"Don't fret," Bernice said as she set a small tray on the bedside table.

Kelsey thought she'd feel embarrassed under the circumstances. They'd brought her back to the ranch and tucked her into Steven's bed, and here was Steven's mother serving her hot tea there.

She felt odd but not embarrassed.

"I'm not used to being waited on," Kelsey said.

Bernice pulled a chair up beside the bed and poured out the beverage. "Nonsense," the older woman said. "There comes a time, now and again, when a woman ought to be waited on." She smiled, and Kelsey realized anew that Bernice was still as beautiful as she appeared in the picture Steven kept on the mantel. Considering that photo had been taken nearly thirty-five years ago, that was certainly saying something.

"I think for some of us," Bernice said, "learning how to graciously accept that pampering and learning how to ask for help when we need it are two of the hardest things to learn in life."

Benny had been put down for a nap, and although he'd protested at first that he wasn't a baby and he wasn't tired, he'd fallen asleep within minutes.

Steven had gone out to the barn once he'd been assured that Benny slept and she, Kelsey, had been made comfortable.

Matthew had headed out to join Adam at the scene of the crash.

Both of her men had been badly shaken by her accident, and she had to admit she had been, too. She'd never encountered anything like what had happened to her on that state road earlier.

She hadn't gotten a real good look at the driver, but the man behind the wheel of that Taurus *had* to have been drunk.

She simply couldn't think of another explanation for what had happened.

Because Mrs. Benedict sat with her, and because she'd lived the last many years without a mother or a motherly friend, Kelsey thought maybe the time had come for her to begin that lesson on how to be gracious while being pampered.

"It's kind of strange having this conversation while I'm in your son's bedroom."

Bernice laughed. "Oh, sweetheart, I know how you feel, but this isn't Steven's bedroom. This is the master bedroom."

Kelsey recalled Steven had said that the first night they'd...well, their first night together. She tilted her head to the side. "Come again?"

"The master bedroom is meant to be shared, Kelsey. When we moved out and turned the house over to Steven, he remained in his own bedroom. Now you're here. This bedroom is as much yours as it is his or Matthew's."

Kelsey felt her jaw drop, then shut her mouth with a snap. "I don't know...I mean, I haven't...that is, I'm not sure what this is between us, let alone where it's going."

"Oh, I know that, sweetheart. You haven't reached the point where you've finally said good-bye to your lost loved ones yet. I understand that. And so, too, do my sons."

Her understanding and that of her sons, come to that, simply floored Kelsey. "I never could have guessed that a place like this would have existed."

"This town was formed to be an oasis. Do you know about the Town Trust?"

Kelsey had heard the expression, but she had no idea what it meant. She shook her head and then closed her eyes as that action hurt.

"All of the land in Lusty is owned by the Town Trust. There's a substantial fortune to see to the needs of the community. Every member of the Benedict, Jessop, and Kendall families has a vote in the trust. Even so, there are things we cannot do. Breaking the covenant that Warren Jessop set up all those years ago is one. So the rules that govern this town stay the same as they were more than a hundred years ago when the town was established. That covenant is simple. People are free to live as they choose, and no laws can be passed to prevent that. In this day and age, such a covenant may not be necessary. You can be certain it was in the eighteen hundreds. Even so, it still stands. "

"So this town is actually all private property, and the Town Trust voted to let me open my restaurant?" Kelsey asked.

"We did. One of the best decisions we've made in recent years if you ask me. Listen to me going on, and here you are not feeling well. You close your eyes and rest. I'll just go downstairs and set the kitchen to rights. I'll come back up and check on you in a while until my boys come back to take over for me."

She'd been enjoying her time with Bernice, but she *was* tired. "Maybe I'll just close my eyes for a few moments." The bed felt so comfortable, she was barely conscious of falling asleep.

It seemed like just minutes later that she opened her eyes to find Matthew sitting beside her where his mother had been.

"Hey." She sat up slowly, waiting for the sledgehammer to start in on her head. It remained silent, but her arms, shoulder, and chest were sore. She inhaled sharply.

"Headache?" Matthew asked.

"No, it's gone."

"Ah, then it has to be the effects of the seat belt. Hot tub would work wonders."

"Hmm, I bet it would, too. If I could get there."

"How about dinner first and then a nice soak?"

"That sounds good. I am a little hungry."

Matthew stood up and then scooped her into his arms. Kelsey squeaked and wrapped her arms around his neck.

"I could probably walk."

"Why walk when you can ride?" He gave her a look that told her it would be useless to argue with him.

She closed her eyes and relaxed, not at all worried that he would drop her. He carried her down the stairs, then down to the end of the hall. She opened her eyes when they reached the kitchen.

Benny greeted her. "Hi, Kelsey!"

How could I have forgotten about Benny? "Hi, Benny. Sorry I've been a little out of it today."

"That's okay. Steven and Granny Bernice took me to see the horses, and then I got some more new toys. Did you get hurt when your car got smashed up? Is that why Matthew is carrying you?"

Steven and Matthew both chuckled. Steven rubbed Benny's head.

"I got just a little bit hurt when my car smashed up," Kelsey said. "Matthew just wanted to carry me to show me how strong he is."

"Matthew said he didn't find my mom yet, but he's getting closer. I told him it's okay. Mom said it might be a while until I see her again."

Kelsey met Matthew's gaze when he set her down on a chair and knew he did have something to report but that he didn't want to do so in front of Benny.

"I hope you're hungry," Steven said. "Mom sent over her famous homemade lasagna fresh from her freezer, and Auntie Anna brought us a Caesar salad and garlic bread."

"I am hungry." She sat quietly while the men served up dinner. She frowned at the amount of pasta Matthew heaped onto her plate. She helped herself to some salad and one piece of garlic bread that smelled entirely too good for her to resist.

"I think that you're probably going to be really sore tomorrow," Steven said. "I was in a car accident once. Like you, I wasn't seriously hurt, but the next day was pure…um, heck."

"I'm afraid you might be right. The doctor did tell me to take it easy for a couple of days. I've already spoken to Tracy. She's going to run the restaurant tomorrow."

"Good," Steven said.

Kelsey couldn't eat much of the delicious dinner. "I'm sorry. I'm sore, and I'm tired."

"I'll take care of the little one. You take care of the big one," Steven said to Matthew.

"Come on, pretty lady," Matthew said. "I'll help you get ready for bed."

Benny scrambled down from his chair and rushed over to give Kelsey a hug. She held him snugly for a long moment, breathing in the familiar scent of a boy who'd played hard all day.

"A bath is on our agenda," Steven assured her.

Kelsey laughed, and Benny groaned.

It didn't take long for Matthew to carry her back to the bedroom. He set her on the bed and then walked out onto the balcony and turned on the heat and jets for the spa.

"While that's getting ready, let's shower." He undressed her, his touch gentle and patient. Then he quickly stripped himself. Kelsey insisted on walking into the bathroom, even though she knew she couldn't hide the stiffness with which she moved.

"Lean on me, sweetheart," Matthew said.

Though she would have characterized herself as independent, she gladly did as he asked. There was no way she'd be able to lift her arms above her head to wash her hair. She didn't need to worry as Matthew took care of that for her.

When they were both clean, he turned off the water, wrapped her hair in a towel, then picked her up and carried her, naked, out to the balcony.

She sighed with pleasure when he climbed into the spa with her and lowered her into the hot, frothing water.

"Oh, God. That feels so good."

"I was right about the bruising," Matthew said. He traced the largest bruise, just above her right breast, with his finger. "It hurts me to see this on you, to know that you're hurting."

She leaned over and kissed him, a gentle, nearly chaste kiss that tasted like more. Then she eased back so she could see his eyes.

"What did you find out today that you didn't want to talk about in front of Benny?"

Matthew sighed. "We've had a bit of a breakthrough on both cases, actually. The Highway Patrol notified us that a car with occupants matching the description of Benny's mom and the man she was with stopped at one of the Pit-Stop service stations just off the state highway about an hour north of here on Sunday evening."

"So they're going to focus their efforts looking in that direction?"

"Yeah. They've begun checking the motels along that route, which leads to Abilene."

"The other development would be about my accident? Did they find that drunk?"

Matthew picked up her hand, kissed it. "The car that ran you off the road is owned by a woman named Mary Peterson, who works as a shop clerk at a discount mall just outside of Waco. The local cops interviewed her at work earlier this afternoon. She'd been at work all day, with witnesses to prove it. However, when she led the cops out to where she'd parked her car, it was gone. They did find it, on mall property."

"You look really worried. What am I missing?"

"The person behind the wheel of that Taurus wasn't drunk, sweetheart. He was trying to kill you."

Chapter 17

"I don't understand. Are you saying that asshole targeted me *specifically?*" Kelsey couldn't wrap her head around what Matthew had just said.

"We believe so, yes. He picked up the Taurus at the mall, likely early this morning. We think he sat and watched, determining which cars belonged to mall employees. Then, of course, he returned it, likely because he'd left his own car there."

"But…who would want to kill me? I haven't done anything!"

Matthew shook his head. He slid closer to Kelsey and stroked a finger down her face. "Baby, we're not going to let anyone hurt you. We have no idea whatsoever why this happened. The Waco police seized the Taurus and are going over it very carefully. That bastard had to have left some evidence. They'll find it. They're also going to go over the mall's security surveillance tapes. In the meantime, until we know what's going on and he's caught, we don't want you going anywhere alone. Okay?"

Kelsey couldn't imagine why someone would deliberately try to harm or kill her. There had to be another explanation. One look at Matthew, though, and the answer to the question he'd just asked seemed obvious. She'd never seen such a serious expression on his face. She recalled the way Steven had looked as he'd taken her out of the cruiser and carried her into the clinic. She didn't want to cause these two good men any unnecessary worry.

"Okay. You're the cop. I'll do whatever you say."

His beautiful smile melted her heart. Amazing that such a simple thing on her part could please him so.

"No more dealing with reality for tonight," Matthew murmured. "Lean back, close your eyes, and let the water, and me, make you feel better."

"I have a real good idea how you could make me feel better," Kelsey said. She sent him a smoldering look. A quick glance down at Matthew's hardening cock told her he thought it was sexy, too.

"So do I, baby. Now relax, close your eyes, and let me take care of you."

The heat of the water and the skill of Matthew's hands as he set about massaging her combined to turn her bones as soft as butter. At least that's how it felt as the tension eased out of her and her stiffened muscles began to relax. She hadn't truly understood how much discomfort she'd been in until it began to ease. Her groans of delight elicited smug masculine chuckles, but she didn't care.

With her eyes closed and her body relaxing, her mind let loose of the questions and the worry. She drifted on the slightest thread of wakefulness, going to that luscious pre-sleep state where sounds muted and melded, cares evaporated, and her spirit soared free.

Matthew lifted her into his arms, and she turned into him, her head seeking the hollow in his collarbone. With her face flush against his chest, she inhaled him. His scent, so masculine right there at the base of his throat, both aroused and soothed her at the same time.

"You're like a sleepy little kitten," Matthew whispered. She felt the soft fluff of a towel against her flesh. A part of her mind knew he dried her and she should probably help. The rest of her decided to just stay in this happy place of care and comfort.

She thought she might be very close to sleep, and although she really wanted to make love with Matthew, she decided that maybe her body needed the sleep more.

"On your tummy, baby," Matthew said.

He helped her so that rolling over didn't take a great deal of effort on her part. Kelsey drifted some more, not really paying any attention to sounds or anything else. The ache in her shoulders had lessened, and lying prone proved comfortable. The brush of cotton against her nude flesh felt wonderful. He must have turned down the bed before he laid her on it. She'd already discovered all the eight hundred thread count linen for this giant double king bed had been made to order. It was the most luxurious bedding she'd ever felt.

Naked male thighs straddled her ass, and her feminine bits began to wake up.

"Something cool," Matthew warned just before he set his hands on her. The scent of lavender teased her. Kelsey recognized her own lotion and sighed as the sensation of Matthew's hands working her back and shoulders continued the process of relaxation.

"You're going to smell like flowers." She heard the slur in her own voice. Speaking had taken a great deal of effort.

"No, darling, I'm going to smell like you."

"Mmm. Am I going to smell like you?" Those words weren't slurred at all.

"Oh, yes. Outside and in, and before long, too."

Such a provocative promise kindled Kelsey's arousal. Before she'd taken Matthew and Steven into her body, she'd believed herself a woman with a fairly low libido. Sex had been good with Philip, warm, tender, and satisfying.

With Matthew and Steven it was all of that and so much more.

Matthew's hands continued to massage her muscles, easing the soreness, relaxing the tension. She loved the weight of him on her bottom, loved the feel of his engorged cock and scrotum resting on her.

This intimacy had nothing to do with sex.

She didn't know what he began to do differently, but relaxation soon gave way to growing arousal. His touch became less firm, more sultry. He trailed his fingers down her side, just brushing by her breast, and her skin turned to gooseflesh. She shivered and felt her nipples drawing in, tightening, so that she had to lift her chest off the bed to center her breasts on the mattress.

"I want you. I want to feel my cock filling your cunt. I want to feel the slide and the glide as I fuck you."

"Yes." Kelsey's slit grew wet, and her hips twitched, then pressed up, seeking more contact between her ass and Matthew's penis. "Yes, I need you to fuck me."

"From behind. I don't want to put my weight on your chest where you're bruised."

"It always feels like more when you fuck me from behind," Kelsey said. The instant Matthew moved back, lifted off her, she spread her legs. The sound of the drawer sliding open and then closed and the foil package being torn open made her juices flow even more.

Matthew moved into place behind her and ran his hand from the small of her back toward her neck until his fingers twined in her hair. She felt his latex-covered cock, the heat and the fullness of it, brush her pussy lips. She moved, wanting to get up on her knees so she could take him deep.

"No, baby. Lie still. I'll take care of you. I'll take care of us both."

He sank into her in one bold stroke, going deep, impossibly deep. A sound of humming pleasure came out of Kelsey's throat. She spread her knees just a little more so that she was completely open to him, offering him everything.

"Christ, you feel so good. So hot and wet and tight around my cock."

"I love having you inside me," Kelsey said. "Harder."

She couldn't say another word. Matthew began thrusting inside her with a force that shook the bed and drove her higher. The tip of his cock pushed against her cervix, and the twinge of pain that caused wrapped around the lust, making her nipples tingle and her clit throb. She loved the climb, the burn and the pinch, the racing heart and heating blood. She loved the sensation of being horny, of being so hot her body began to feel desperate to come.

"Oh, please." Kelsey knew she could beg and that begging would never be used against her. When Matthew responded by slowing his thrusts, by tempering them so he didn't drive as deep, she whimpered.

"Do you want to come, baby?"

"Yes. Please. Make me come."

"Mmm. I love the feel of your pussy clenching around my cock as your orgasm takes you. Of course, I love the way it feels when you squeeze me, too. Do that for me now, baby. Squeeze my cock with those wonderful muscles of yours."

Kelsey squeezed him, the long-ago learned Kegel exercises making Matthew sound nearly as desperate as she.

Matthew responded by resuming his hot and heavy rhythm. Kelsey gripped his cock, tightening all her inner muscles, holding him and holding off the pending explosion.

"Give it to me, baby. Come on my cock."

Oh, God. The shivers and tingles wouldn't stay where she kept them, wouldn't stay down and small. They surged, out of control. Crying out, Kelsey pushed back against Matthew as the explosion shattered her control. She came with such fierce convulsions she could see stars behind her eyes, every nerve ending in her body sizzling as if she'd been hit by lightning.

"Yeah. Oh, Kelsey, *yes.*" Matthew's orgasm took him as he held himself deep. One arm slipped under her and around her, pulling her into him. The sensation of his ejaculation into the condom against her cervix made her own climax spike again. She squealed, a high-pitched sound of pleasure so sharp, she wondered she could make such a sound.

The heat of his body against her back as he held himself just off her became a wonderful blanket. His heavy gasps for breath tickled her ear. She focused on breathing.

"Did I hurt you, sweetheart?"

"Nuh." She didn't have a hope of forming a coherent word, let alone a sentence. Matthew's kissed her shoulder then left his face nestled there, and she felt him smile.

"So, I fucked you senseless, did I?"

"Mmm." She smiled, too, and in that moment, she felt that nothing bad could happen, nothing could touch her, because this man and his brother loved her.

"Ah, that scene reminds me of this morning."

At the sound of Steven's voice, Kelsey turned her head to the side and opened her eyes. Steven stood at the doorway, a smile on his face.

"Did you feel like a train wreck after loving her, too?" Matthew asked his brother.

"Hell, yes. No woman has ever taken me apart and put me back together again the way our Kelsey does."

Matthew kissed her neck, then slid off her, claiming the right side of the bed as he had every night they'd slept together.

Kelsey eased onto her back so she could better watch Steven as he moved around the room.

"Benny is clean and tucked into his bed. I read him one story, and he fell asleep before I was done." Steven checked that the volume of the monitor had been turned up, then came over to the bed. He dropped his clothes in a heap on the floor, Kelsey had noticed he tended to do this but always picked them up the next morning, then slid into bed on her left.

"How are you feeling?" Steven turned to face her and propped his head up on his right hand. Like his brother had, he gently traced the bruise on her shoulder, then moved down to the smaller ones on her hip.

She decided not to sugarcoat her answer. "Still a bit sore, but not as bad as when I woke up before dinner."

"Might be really sore tomorrow," Matthew cautioned.

"Yes, I know. There is just one more thing, though. Under the heading of how I feel."

"What?"

Both men asked that at once. Kelsey fought back a smile. She lay on her back with the Benedict brothers now half propped up over her, one on each side. The perfect position, she thought, for seeing both their expressions at the same time.

"I love you." She looked at each of them in turn. "I love you both. I'm not sure what I'm going to do about it or what our future is yet. But I do love you."

Their smiles reminded her of lilies in bloom, and Kelsey felt love unfurling in her heart, warming every bit of her.

"It's about damn time," Matthew grumbled. When he kissed her, the caress was gentle.

"You can say that again," Steven echoed. He kissed her just as gently, and then they both just grinned like fools.

"That's the first step, baby. We both sure as hell love you," Steven said.

"Let's just take things one day at a time," Matthew said.

Kelsey wondered then if they didn't know her better than she knew herself. She'd said she had no idea what the future held for them, but the men didn't seem to have any doubts at all.

* * * *

Connors had known there was a good reason he'd left his fledgling career in larceny behind. Being a crook was just too damn nerve-wracking, not to mention the fact that he wasn't really very good at it. At least he hadn't been today.

When he heard the siren and seen that cop car come over that hill in his rearview mirror, he'd nearly shit his pants. He had his gun in one hand and the door handle in the other. Instead of moving on the Madison woman, though, he slammed the car back into drive and floored it. Of course, the cop had to stop and see if anyone was hurt first, but cops had radios. He hadn't stopped shaking until he'd been back in his own vehicle and headed for home.

Connors drove aimlessly through the streets of Austin. He stopped for an early dinner at a burger joint, and by the time he finished his fries and cola, had nearly gotten his cool back. He'd pulled over at a service station in Waco and removed the disguise he'd worn for the morning's adventure. No one had noticed him going into the washroom wearing a cap and moustache and coming out without them. He ditched both items there, shoving them deep into the trash can.

He hadn't planned to run the woman off the road. That had been an act of opportunity. When he'd seen her car hit the tree, he figured it was a good sign. It would have been easier to put a bullet in her head while she was unconscious.

The gun was a holdover from his life of crime, a Glock he'd gotten from a friend of a friend that could never be traced to him. After doing what he had to do to protect the new life he'd built for himself, he'd planned to dump the gun in the Brazos River.

Connors ran a hand through his hair. He had no idea how badly the woman had been hurt, and he had no fucking idea what the hell he was going to do now.

It was nearly nine. Cora Lynn would be calling soon. He'd check the local news stations and cruise the web. Somewhere there would be a report on the woman's accident, especially if they'd put out an APB on the Taurus.

Thank God he'd been smart enough to steal a car.

He hit the remote for his garage as he neared his house. The neighborhood was as quiet as it usually was on a Monday evening. There was a nice mix of ages here. Some of his neighbors were retired, some newlyweds. Of course they all knew him. Connors was the neighborhood go-to man if anyone needed help with anything. He'd cultivated that persona here at home and at work in the real estate office.

He turned off the car, locked it, and headed into the house. He immediately heard voices and realized the television was on in his den. He didn't think he'd left the thing on, but he might have.

His mind still on Kelsey Madison and his problem, he walked down the hall and then froze at the door to his den. Sherman Fremont sat in his recliner.

"There you are, Connors. You get points for eluding the police. But you really should have come to me with this problem rather than trying to handle it yourself."

"Mr. Fremont."

"Come in, Connors. Make yourself at home." Sherman Fremont laughed at his joke, but the man who stood behind him giving a good imitation of a gorilla didn't laugh.

"I don't understand—"

"I told you I liked the looks of you, and I meant it. And you may not understand right now, but you will, that this is one of the things I liked about you. I knew about this particular skeleton in your closet.

"It doesn't always take money to buy a politician, Connors. Come and sit down. I'm about to buy you. Johnson, here, will help you with the Madison woman."

Chapter 18

"It'll likely be a couple of days before we hear anything back from the Waco P.D.," Matthew said.

"Let's hope that s.o.b. left behind enough evidence that you can find him," Steven said.

"Yeah, I'm hoping," Matthew agreed.

Steven got up to bring the coffee pot to the kitchen table. Kelsey looked as if she was lost in thought, and Matthew looked as if he wanted to spit nails.

I can't blame him.

Steven felt just as helpless at the moment.

The need to protect Kelsey surged through his veins. He wanted to punch someone very badly. It was hard to fight an enemy he couldn't see.

"How are you feeling this morning, sweetheart?" he asked Kelsey. He'd gotten up just before dawn, leaving the bed to get his morning chores done while his lover and his brother still slept. Then he'd come into the house to find breakfast ready to be served and Benny ready to chatter. The little guy had plowed through his morning meal and now played quietly.

"I'm a little stiff and sore, but it's not as bad as I thought it would be." She blinked and looked over at him. "Don't worry. I'm not going into the restaurant today even though I don't feel as bad as I anticipated."

The sound of toy trucks crashing into each other came from the sitting room. Steven could look over top of the kitchen counter and see the Benny's head. He understood now why his mother had insisted on an "open concept" for the main living areas of kitchen and parlor when his parents renovated this house. It was nice to be able to see what the boy was doing without having to keep getting up to do so.

"You'll want to go in tomorrow, though," Matthew said. "Don't get me wrong, there's nothing Steven and I would like better than to lock you up somewhere and keep you safe. We know we can't do that."

Kelsey tilted her head to the side and looked at Matt and then at him. "What do I need to do so that the two of you won't get sick worrying about me?"

"You just did it," Steven said. Thinking about her past, he leaned forward and kissed her. Then he chose his words carefully. "When you love someone, you're always hostage to their fortune. It goes with the territory. We know you take our concerns seriously. That has to be enough. The rest is our problem."

The phone rang, and Steven got up to answer it.

"Hi, Mom. We're just finishing breakfast."

"I thought I'd come over around lunch time and spend a bit of time with Benny," his mother said. "Get in some grandma practice and give you and Kelsey a chance to have some time to yourselves. I know how challenging it can be to suddenly have a child there when you're not used to children."

"That would be great, Mom. See you when you get here."

"I knew Mom would take every opportunity to spend time with him," Matthew said when Steven came back to the table.

Steven laughed. Since Kelsey looked confused, he said, "Mom has been dropping not-so-subtle-hints for the last couple of years that she wants a *lot* of grandchildren."

"She'll make a wonderful granny. She was so great with Benny yesterday," Kelsey said. "I think they both just clicked right from the first moment. Love at first sight."

"I think they did, too. So when Mom gets here, do you want to go riding?"

Kelsey grinned. "I haven't been riding for several years. I'm probably rusty, but yeah, I'd like to."

"I have a mare that I use for some of the less experienced riders in the family. She's pretty gentle, really."

A cell phone rang, and Matthew pulled the device off his belt and looked at the call display before answering.

"Hey, Adam. I was finishing breakfast and then—" Matthew stopped talking, and Steven could see by the expression on his brother's face that something had happened.

"Okay, I'll head out from here and pick you up. No sense in our taking two cars. Just give me five." Matthew closed his cell phone and looked to see what Benny was doing. Then he turned to Steven and Kelsey.

"Rangers got a call from the manager of a motel just outside of Coleman in response to the BOLO they issued yesterday. So they responded, and now they have one Deke Walters in custody."

"And Benny's mother?" Kelsey asked quietly.

Matthew, once more, checked to see the little boy was busy playing and not paying the adults any attention before he turned a somber face to them.

"She wasn't with him. She's missing."

* * * *

Kelsey paid close attention as Steven saddled the mare. It had been several years since she'd last sat a horse. As she watched him work, the process of readying a mount to ride came back to her. As she stood inside the neat barn, time seemed to melt away. The scent of horse and hay had once been her favorite aroma.

She'd taken riding lessons when she'd been a horse-mad twelve-year-old girl growing up in northeastern Pennsylvania. She'd saved her allowance all winter, plus did odd jobs for her elderly neighbor, Mrs. Pierce, so that come the summer she could take those lessons and spend time with her equine friends.

When she'd married Philip and moved to Austin, she'd found a riding stable outside of the city and resumed the pastime. That had been just one more thing that had been lost in the aftermath of the trauma five years before.

"I suppose if I hadn't been such a hard-ass about trying to keep the relationship between the three of us just about sex, I could have gone riding weeks ago."

Steven looked up, his grin wide. "Darlin', you and I both know there's no way I can comment on that statement and win. So I'm just going to smile and say you look lovely today."

"You're a pretty smart man," Kelsey said. There was so much about the brothers Benedict that she liked and admired. Their quick minds ranked up near the top of the list.

"My momma didn't raise no fools," Steven said with an exaggerated twang.

Kelsey laughed. Then the smile died as she thought again about Matthew's phone call of just minutes before.

The state cops as well as Matthew and Adam had questioned Deke Walters. He claimed he had no idea where Benny's mom had gone. "Where do you think Ginny Rose is?"

"My guess is she's going to try and find her way back here," Steven said

"That's what I think, too. Matthew sounded disappointed when that trucker stepped forward to say he saw her leave the motel room and take off across the field. I think he wanted to keep Deke in custody."

"Can you blame him, really? Judging by the letter Ginny left, Deke Walters put his hands on her on a regular basis. The man likely deserves to spend some time in jail. Unfortunately, he doesn't deserve to be charged with Ginny's disappearance."

Kelsey had no tolerance for anyone who abused someone smaller or weaker than themselves. She didn't know anything about Walters but could easily picture him, a big bruiser of a guy in a wife-beater T-shirt holding a can of beer while playing armchair quarterback.

"Let's hope someone sees her and soon. It's a long way from that motel back to here." Kelsey knew she'd worry about the woman until she was found.

"On top of the distance, there's the danger of just being out in open country. She's a city gal and likely doesn't have a clue how to survive in the wilderness."

They'd decided not to say anything to Benny. Not until they had something positive to report to him. For the most part, the little boy seemed happy. He certainly loved all the new toys the people of Lusty had given to him, and he enjoyed the attention they were lavishing on him. Yet there were moments when his little lip quivered, and Kelsey knew he really wanted his mother.

"Come on, sweetheart. There's nothing we can do for Benny right now. Mom's taking good care of him," Steven said.

The tenderness in his expression and in his voice told her more than his actual words how attuned he was to her. She'd never believed men could be so macho and so caring at the same time until she'd taken up with these Benedict brothers.

"I know you're right."

Steven handed her the reins of her horse, a chestnut mare named Daisy. When he offered her a leg up, she accepted, swinging her right leg over the horse.

"That hurt," Steven said as she settled herself in the saddle.

He'd obviously seen her wince. She wasn't going to lie to him. "Just lifting my own weight hurt my arm and shoulder a bit. It's all right. I can't baby it too much, or it'll just get even more painful and stiffen up to boot."

"I know. Damn it. I hate like hell that you're in pain."

Steven swung up on the back of his black gelding. Kelsey thought both man and beast appeared strong, arrogant, and in charge of the world.

The brothers had been careful to make sure she knew they respected her right to be an independent woman. She also had no doubts whatsoever that they each had definite limits in mind for that independence and would do what they felt necessary to take care of her and keep her safe.

It surprised her some that she was okay with that.

"Did you read the story of how the Benedicts came to be settled on this land?" Steven asked as the horses began to move.

"Didn't Sarah bring the ranch into the family when she married Caleb Benedict? She'd been widowed, hadn't she?"

Steven raised both eyebrows as he shot her a teasing look. "You only skimmed the barest amount of information when we took you to the museum, didn't you?"

"You expected me to read and retain when I was still trying to adjust to the fact that you and your brother wanted to share me? When all the hormones in my body were jumping up and down with fevered excitement, yelling at me to strip and get started?"

Steven grinned. "We got to you right away, did we?" He brought his horse to a stop, and she mimicked the move. Then he leaned over and kissed her quickly. He sat back, apparently not really expecting an answer. "I suppose for someone who didn't grow up in Lusty, the concept would be a strange one."

"You think?" Kelsey asked.

Steven only laughed and clucked at his horse.

Kelsey followed him as he led the way away from the house and barns out into the open fields of the ranch. "I only employ a handful of men now," Steven said, "as the ranch is more of a tradition than anything else. Most of the family's wealth comes from investments, land and property development, and manufacturing businesses purchased over the years. And then there's the oil, of course."

"Of course."

"Actually, I think it could be said that oil was the foundation of the whole damn thing."

When he didn't say any more, Kelsey fell silent, wondering if she was going to have to drag the story out of him. He led her to a small hillock or one that looked small. Once they were on top of it, he brought his horse to a halt and turned in his saddle. When she turned her gaze in the direction he indicated, she gasped, for she could see the big house, and the "new house," and most of Lusty.

"When Caleb, Joshua, and Sarah moved into the big house, it was shortly after the death of its owner, a man named Maddox. Maddox had struck a business deal with Sarah's father for her hand in marriage. They discovered after several attempts were made on her life that Maddox had married Sarah solely for the inheritance left to her by her paternal grandfather. He'd planned to have her killed to get it."

"That's horrible! Oh, I'm so glad I didn't live in those days. Why, women were little more than chattel in the eighteen hundreds!"

"That's a fact," Steven said. "Anyway, in the end Maddox died at the hand of Joshua Benedict, and Sarah inherited his entire estate as well as the one left to her by her grandfather."

"I'll bet she shared it with her men," Kelsey said.

"You'd win that bet."

Daisy responded well to Sarah's guidance. "I've missed this. I really love riding."

"Matt and I would go out as often as we could when we were kids. Since he came back home from Chicago, we've picked up the habit again. Most Sundays we go for a nice long ride. This next Sunday, we'll all three go together."

"What was she like? Matthew's wife?"

"I only met her once, and I didn't like her. I think he fell in lust with her, and she fell in lust with the family fortune."

"Huh." Kelsey never gave much thought to the fact that the Benedicts were extremely wealthy. Knowing Susan as she did, it was hard to think of the Benedicts as being rich.

"Matthew refers to the years he was in Chicago as his rebellious stage." Steven stopped then, his gaze somber. "I thought I'd never get the chance to meet you."

What an odd thing to say. Kelsey turned to ask him what he meant when a gunshot exploded, kicking dust up by her horse's hooves.

* * * *

"The Rangers are going to send an alert to the truck stops and service centers between Coleman and here," Adam said. "Beyond that, there's not much we can do to find Ginny."

They entered Lusty city limits, and in moments, Matthew pulled the cruiser to the curb in front of the sheriff's office.

"I'll follow up, speak to some of them by phone," Matthew said as he got out of the car. "Let them know Ginny isn't a criminal. I don't want them spooking her away."

Once inside the building, Adam went to his desk, tossing his hat on the rack as he passed. "Matt. There are a lot of people who think that when a mother deserts her son, it's a pretty criminal act."

Matthew looked over at his best friend and understood that Adam wasn't seeing the situation the same way that he, Steven, and Kelsey were.

"She was in an impossible situation and did what she could to keep her son safe. The little guy was clean, healthy, and happy. He's not an abused kid, Adam. Every indication is that Ginny loves Benny and has been a good mother to him. I think Ginny left Deke because the reality of having given her son up got through to her like nothing else could."

Adam scrubbed his hands over his face. "Okay. That letter pretty much speaks to her intent. I guess we'll have to wait and see. If she shows up here, we'll talk to her and then reassess the situation."

"Thanks. We feel pretty strongly about this. Kelsey does, especially."

He sat down at his own desk and turned on his computer. First, he'd check his e-mail and then he'd contact the Waco police. Just before they drove over to Coleman, the Waco PD called Adam and told him they had seized the mall's surveillance tapes. Matthew was hoping they'd had some luck there.

As soon as he saw the e-mail from the Austin P.D., Matthew opened it. He'd nearly forgotten about the request he'd put in to Patrick Carmichael yesterday. The detective had sent the case file as a download attachment.

Matthew hadn't expected any surprises as he read, but he got a couple of them. The first rocked him.

"She witnessed the shooting." He looked over at Adam when that man swore and didn't wonder that he didn't have to explain himself.

"No wonder it took her so long to open up about it."

"I thought she meant that she'd just waited outside in the car when it happened and saw them after the gunman escaped. But she actually saw it happen." Matthew kept reading.

He got his second shock, and this one made all the pieces fall in to place.

"Son of a bitch. I know who's trying to kill her."

Before he could explain to Adam, his cell phone rang. He looked at the call display. Seeing his brother's name inexplicably sent a chill down his spine.

Chapter 19

Kelsey refused to go back to the house. She knew neither Steven nor Matt were happy with her implacability. That was just too damn bad.

She wasn't too happy about Steven's refusal to go to the clinic either.

"It's only a graze, honey. I'm fine." He'd hugged her, and she'd finally started breathing again. Eventually, the internal shaking had stopped. Then the fear disintegrated under a barrage of red, hot fury.

Some son-of-a-bitch had taken a couple of shots at them, wounding Steven.

Her gaze found her men among the twenty or so people combing the slight rise on the edge of town between the general store and the ranchland. Matthew's brown uniform stood out, as did Steven's hastily bandaged arm.

She sat in the back of Matthew's cruiser, with one of his fathers in the front seat and the other in the back beside her.

"Unless that bastard picked up his shell casings, they should be finding something soon," Caleb Benedict said.

"Sorry son-of-a-bitch better not show his face around here again. The women alone would beat him to bloody death for threatening two of our own," Jonathan Benedict said.

"Damn right," Caleb agreed.

Kelsey felt warmth suffuse her at those words. She turned to Jonathan, who sat beside her.

"You need to insist your son sees the doctor."

Both men smiled. "Don't you worry, sweetheart," Jonathan said. "As soon as they find the evidence, Bernice will see to it if he doesn't."

"He's doing what he can to take care of you," Caleb said. "That's the Benedict way. Once they've finished their search, he'll head on over because you asked him to."

"I'm sorry he got hurt. I don't understand why anyone would try—"

"Now, sweetheart, if you're apologizing, you can stop right there. None of this is your fault. It's the fault of the man who pulled that trigger," Jonathan said.

"And the fault of the man who sent him," Caleb said.

"You think someone…"

"The first attempt was some asshole, pardon my language, behind the wheel of a car running you off the road and the second a sniper attack. Speaks to two separate M.O.'s." Caleb said.

Since Caleb had been a Texas Ranger, she guessed he knew what he was talking about. She turned her attention back to the men. Steven held up his hand, and everyone seemed to stop. Adam and Matthew both came over to him. Matt got down on his knees beside his brother. A few seconds later, he held up what looked like a baggie with something in it.

"Good." Caleb turned to Kelsey. "Now they'll be able to know what caliber bullet, and from that, the make and model of gun. If they seize the weapon, they'll be able to prove it was the one used because they have that casing."

Matthew handed the bag to Adam, then came toward the car. He leaned in through the open back window and placed a kiss on Kelsey's face.

"We've done all we can going over where the shooter stood," Matthew said. "Adam's going to get all the volunteers together, see if their canvass turned up any descriptions of the perp. In the mean time, we need to talk. Since Mom's still with Benny at the ranch, let's head over to the big house."

"Certainly," Kelsey said. "Just as soon as one of the doctors over at the clinic has a look at Steven's arm and gives him a proper bandage."

* * * *

It seemed the most natural thing in the world to Steven to worry about his woman and do everything in his power to protect her and keep her safe. Being the recipient of that same treatment was something else again.

He'd known she'd been taken back to that other shooting five years before. That knowledge had kept his voice calm, his actions gentle even as he'd wanted to swear with the pain from his wound. He did his best to downplay his injury. He hadn't lied to her. He really had only been grazed. But it hurt like hell.

"There," Dr. Adam Jessop said as he smoothed the bandage into place. "Cleaned, disinfected, and antibiotic cream applied. I imagine it stings like hell." He raised one eyebrow, and even though Kelsey sat next to him and he wanted to spare her, he never could lie to his Uncle Adam.

"It stings," he said.

Steven felt himself scowl when Dr. Adam looked over at Kelsey. "I'll give him a prescription for Tylenol with codeine." He went over to the PC that sat on the counter in the exam room. The clinic had gone to computers a few years back, which made the pharmacist in town happy as all prescriptions were now printed out and legible.

"And it appears you need a tetanus booster."

"Well, hell," Steven said.

Kelsey leaned in and kissed his shoulder. "Sorry, sweetheart."

He looked over at Matthew who stood on the other side of Kelsey. His brother's smirk grounded him as much as Kelsey's affection soothed him.

"Just a pinch."

Steven wondered why doctors always said that before jabbing those big ass needles into his arm and twisting them every which way. At least it felt as if they did. Uncle Adam gave him the shot in his left arm. Steven supposed it was better than having to stand and lower his pants, but not by much.

He couldn't help the slight hiss as he inhaled sharply.

"F…ooey, that hurts."

"It was just a little pinch," Dr. Adam reiterated. Steven noted the twinkle in the man's eyes.

It was a sad world, Steven thought, when your own doctor, who was also a family member, laughed at your pain.

"Come on, tough guy. By now the dads will have the coffee made and some of Mom's cookies out," Matthew said.

"One day, it will be your turn in here," Steven said to his brother. "And I will remember your lack of sympathy."

"Men," Kelsey said, "are such babies."

It took only a few minutes to drive over to the big house. When he'd been a kid, this was where they came for Sunday dinner to visit Grandpa Pat and Grandpa Gerald and Grandma Kate. His grandfathers were gone, but Grandma Kate was still alive, and about four years ago, his fathers had retired from ranching, turned the operation over to him, and moved with his mother into the big house.

He'd never lived here, but it always had felt like home.

As he suspected, his fathers were in the dining room, setting out refreshments. When they stopped ranching, they both decided to learn how to cook and bake to give their wife a break—so that she could, in effect, share in the concept of retirement.

Already comfortable at the table and happily eating some cookies, Lusty's sheriff nodded to him when they came into the room.

While they'd been combing the grass looking for those shell casings, Matthew had told him what he'd learned just moments before Steven had called him.

"Sit down, Steven. I'll pour you some coffee," Kelsey said.

"I've got it, sweetheart. You sit down and take it easy, now." Jonathan waved her into a chair. Steven sat on one side of her and Matthew the other. Matt turned his chair slightly so that he faced her.

"How's the shoulder?" Matthew asked her.

"Sore. Coming off Daisy and rolling on the ground to get behind those rocks wasn't fun, but it sure as hell beat the alternative. I forgot," Kelsey turned to Steven. "How are the horses?"

Both mounts had run off, spooked by the gunfire. Steven was pleased to give Kelsey one bit of good news anyway. "They made it back to the barn. Jim, one of the hands, checked them over. Not a scratch. They're both fine."

"That's a relief." Then she turned her attention to Matthew. "Your mom's all right staying with Benny a little longer? I just feel like we should—"

"Kelsey."

Steven knew it was Matthew's tone that got Kelsey to stop talking. He shared a look with his brother. Their woman was nervous, as if she knew she wasn't going to like whatever it was Matthew was going to say to her.

"Yes, Matthew?" Kelsey said.

"Sweetheart, we need to talk."

* * * *

Kelsey didn't know why she felt so damn nervous. Maybe it was part of an adrenaline crash. In a few short hours, she'd gone from being in a great mood, to terror, then worry, to fury. There'd only been one time before like it, and she really didn't want to think about that other time right now.

But it was time for her to pull up her big girl panties and hear whatever Matthew needed to tell her. She couldn't afford to hide or withdraw from reality. That bullet had only grazed Steven, but it so easily could have killed him.

Inside her head a voice of rebellion whispered, this is why it's a bad idea to get involved with anyone. People you love get hurt, and sometimes they die.

Kelsey ignored that voice. It was already too late. She'd become involved with the brothers Benedict. She'd found love under two Benedicts, and she would not, could not, go back.

"All right. I just know I'm not going to like this." She inhaled deeply. Then she let the air out and nodded.

"We know there've been two attempts now aimed at you. We couldn't figure out why, so it didn't make any sense. Kelsey, this afternoon the Austin P.D. sent me the file on Philip and Sean's deaths."

Kelsey felt her heart sink. "They killed the man who did that. His face was caught on the store's surveillance camera. Then the police closed in, and there was a gunfight and he died." Kelsey stopped for a moment, steadied herself. Beside her, Steven moved closer, and put his hand on her shoulder.

That simple touch helped.

"There was absolutely no doubt he was the one," Kelsey said.

"All that is true. But the authorities never caught the second man."

"There was no second man." She'd said that automatically. At the time, the Austin police had told her there had been a second man, a getaway driver. They'd questioned her because they'd believed she'd seen this man.

According to the police, he'd been behind the wheel of a car that had also been in the store's parking lot.

"Sweetheart? I need you to listen to me, and I need you to believe me. The Austin police never pushed the matter because of the trauma you suffered. However, that store had two cameras, one inside, one outside. The outside camera clearly shows you in your car *and* shows the getaway car. He was parked right in front of you, facing you. It wasn't even full dark out, so you must have seen him."

"I…" Kelsey was shaking inside, and she couldn't seem to stop it. "I really don't remember seeing him."

"I believe you," Matthew said.

"Sometimes, when we witness horrific things, our subconscious will take over and edit our memory of the event," Steven said. "I think the moment you witnessed your family being murdered, your subconscious just shut your mind off for a little bit."

"I remember seeing them shot, and then the next thing I remember is being at the hospital." No one said anything. Steven's arm had come all the way around her, and Matthew held both her hands, his thumbs rubbing the backs of them. In that moment, it felt as if the world only contained her, Steven, and Matthew.

"You think the getaway driver is the person trying to kill me now?" Kelsey asked.

"Yes, I do."

"Why now? It's been five years."

"I don't have an answer for that," Matthew said.

"Maybe he got sent up for something else and only came out of the system," Adam said. "There was that newspaper interview you did about the restaurant. The reporter dedicated a few paragraphs to your past and how you'd found triumph after tragedy. That's how Benny's mom picked you for her son. Maybe that's what drew his attention to you, too."

"If so, he might have been hanging around the restaurant a time or two, getting an idea of your routine," Caleb said.

"In any event, keeping you safe may hinge on you remembering what that guy looked like," Matthew said.

"I just draw a blank," Kelsey said. Her nerves had eased, and the shaking stopped. She wrapped her hands around Matthew's and leaned into Steven's embrace.

"By yourself," Matthew agreed. "Under hypnosis, you might remember everything."

"You want me to submit to hypnosis?"

Matthew squeezed her hands. "I want you to think about it. We need to stop this guy, honey. We need to keep you safe."

"One of your dads said this attack had a different M. O. than the one with the car." Kelsey felt as if she grasped at straws. In her heart, she knew Matthew was right. She knew she should just say yes, she'd do the hypnosis thing, but a part of her fought reality.

"Caleb's right," Adam said. "It just means the asshole hired someone."

"Why?" Kelsey asked again. "It's been five years."

"If we catch him, and he's convicted as an accessory to murder, sweetheart, he could get the death penalty," Matthew said.

No one said anything for a long moment, letting her have the silence. No one looked at her as though he thought she was being foolish. And she knew if she said no to the hypnosis, then that would be the end of it.

"I'll think about it. The concept scares me, but I'll think about it."

"Good girl." Matthew leaned forward and kissed her.

"I'm taking the shell casings into Waco. Their lab can tell us what we need to know," Adam said. "I suspect a high-powered sniper weapon."

"Isn't that a kind of rare gun?" Kelsey asked.

"This is Texas," Adam said. "We have every sort of gun under the damn sun here."

"Oh. What about the canvass?" Kelsey recalled that one of the dads had said some of the townsfolk had volunteered to ask others if they'd seen any unfamiliar vehicles in the area at the time of the shooting.

"My brother Morgan organized that," Adam said, then he smiled. "Hell of a welcome home for him. Steps foot in town and immediately gets drafted. I'll be getting the report when I go back to the office." Then he looked at Matthew. "You head on home now. Take care of your woman."

Kelsey bristled just a little. She raised one eyebrow and skewered Lusty's sheriff with as stern a look as she could muster. The man simply smiled and winked at her. She wondered then if he'd said that just to get a rise out of her.

"I'm not going to sit around in case he changes his mind," Matthew said as he got to his feet.

The brothers Benedict would have rushed her out the door in seconds, but Kelsey insisted on thanking the dads not only for the coffee and cookies, but for sitting with her while the others gathered evidence. When each man, in turn, gave her a very tight hug, she thought she just might start to cry.

"Come on, sweetheart," Steven said.

They got in Matthew's cruiser. Kelsey insisted on sitting in the back seat, thinking the front would be easier for Steven with his injured arm.

"It's just a graze," he said to her. "And when we get home, I'll prove it."

For the first time in a couple of hours, Kelsey felt her spirit lighten. "Is that a fact?"

Matthew met her gaze in the rearview mirror. "Fair warning. Once Benny is asleep, you're going to be in for it. What do you have to say about that, darlin'?"

Kelsey would have thought her hunger and need for these two men would have abated by now, or at least leveled off. Instead, they had a knack for making her wet with just their words. She felt wanted, and loved, and most definitely aroused.

Kelsey smiled. "Bring it on, deputy. Bring it on."

Chapter 20

The promise of private time and the decadent pleasures that would bring kept Kelsey's blood humming all evening. Benny was delighted to see them all home at the same time. When he saw the bandage on Steven's arm, he asked if he'd fallen off his horse.

Since that seemed the easiest answer to give the inquisitive four-year-old, he said yes.

It was all she and Matthew could do after that not to laugh. No one delivered pitying looks the way a small child could.

They fired up the outdoor grill and cooked hamburgers for dinner. Steven redeemed himself in Benny's eyes by playing with him and his fleet of trucks on the back lawn while Matthew manned the grill. They had so much fun that, after dinner, Matthew joined them.

Kelsey wondered if that was just an elaborate ploy on the part of the men to get out of after-dinner clean up. Since they did seem to enjoy playing with the little guy, she really didn't mind.

Kelsey could see them from the kitchen window as she finished up the dishes. Hearing Benny laugh and watching the way both grown men were able to relate to him filled Kelsey's heart.

They'll make very good fathers.

When the males came into the house, chased by encroaching darkness, Kelsey scooped up Benny and took him upstairs for his bath. He seemed to enjoy the water, especially when he could have boats to captain. Kelsey smiled as he made different engine sounds for each one.

He didn't argue about brushing his teeth. When she tucked him into bed, he begged for a story. Kelsey complied, but as she expected he would, he fell asleep before even a couple of pages had been read.

She sat for a moment in the chair beside his bed, watching him sleep, the stuffed walrus clutched tight. All through the evening, through dinner, then a bath, then a story, she'd felt echoes of the past, echoes of Sean.

There would always be a hole in her heart because he was gone. But the sharp edge of grief that even so recently had slashed at her seemed less somehow.

She'd opened her heart to this child and to the brothers Benedict, and she thought that she was beginning to understand. It wasn't time that could heal all wounds. It was love.

Sounds coming from across the hall told her the men had come upstairs. She took one more moment to smooth the blankets over Benny and to give him a tiny kiss on his head.

Then she went across the hall, ready for her own nighttime routine.

They'd turned off the lights. She watched them, both shirtless, as they went about turning on soft music and turning down the bed.

Though she'd entered the room silently, they both looked up at her at the same moment. They wore twin expressions of longing and lust and love.

Right then, Kelsey understood that for these two brothers it had *never* been just about sex. Bernice had said this room belonged to the three of them equally. Built large enough for four adults, she knew of a couple of families where the husbands numbered three, this bedroom in this house was meant to be a sanctuary for love. An old-fashioned concept, the marriage bed, had kept this room empty until these men had brought her here.

Until she'd arrived that first night.

A town founded on the fundamental ideal that freedom meant freedom to love, and to live, as a person chose. This town was filled with families, descendents of the original founders, who stood with open arms and open hearts not just for their own, but for those who needed them and those who made this town their own. This was their heritage. How had she ever gotten so lucky as to come here?

"Can you tell us what you're thinking to put that beautiful expression on your face, sweetheart?" Matthew asked.

"I will if you'll answer a question for me. How many divorces have there been in your family?"

Steven raised one eyebrow. And then he smiled as if he understood her thoughts completely.

"Just Benedicts? Or Benedicts, Kendalls, Jessops, Parkers, and Joneses?"

"All of them."

"Of the family members who remained here in Lusty, none."

Kelsey smiled. "That's what I thought."

"That thought couldn't have been the author of that smile," Matthew said. "Your eyes sparkled with love."

"Because I was thinking about how much I love you both. I was thinking about how profoundly grateful I am that I came here and that you were waiting for me."

"Sweetheart."

Until they came to her, until each reached out to brush her cheeks, she didn't realize tears streaked down her face.

"I love you, Kelsey. I never knew I could love anyone this much. It's only been a few weeks but already it feels as if you're a part of me." Steven's words melted her heart. She leaned in, leaned up, and laid her lips on his. Reverence reverberated in her kiss, the touch light yet trembling with love.

She straightened and turned to Matthew when he stroked her arm.

"I love you, Kelsey. The first moment I laid eyes on you, I knew, deep down, you were meant to be ours. That first time you laid with us here my world finally came right."

As she had with Steven, she kissed Matthew, showing him how deeply his words had touched her. When she straightened, she said, "I need you, both of you, inside me. I want to be so full of you that I can't tell where you end and I begin."

"Yes, we want you naked between us," Matthew said.

She wanted them naked, too. She wanted to reach out, undress them, and caress each new bit of flesh she uncovered, but they had a different idea.

With movements fast and economical, they stripped the clothes from her, baring her body to their sight and their touch. Her nipples became hard pebbles as first gazes and then fingers touched and teased. Matthew bent to suck one hard peak into his mouth while Steven turned her face toward him. He kissed her, his lips hot and wet, his mouth opening wide over hers, claiming her. His tongue swept her mouth, drank her, and Kelsey wanted nothing more than to submit to him, to give him whatever he wanted.

Matthew brushed his hand over the hot, swollen flesh above her slit, and her knees buckled.

"You are so incredibly responsive to us, baby," he sighed.

"She was made for us," Steven said.

"We were made for each other," Kelsey said.

Matthew lifted her and laid her on the bed. Their gazes never left her as they shucked the rest of their clothes. With their corded muscles, chests sprinkled with hair, cocks erect with desire for her, she would never get over how beautiful they were, the two of them.

And they were all hers.

Her cunt flooded with the dew of her own desire as they came to her. Lips and hands, tongues and fingers, they tasted, they touched, they took. Kelsey took as well. She stroked and gripped, cupped and caressed. No words were needed here as bodies, hot, aroused, and attuned spoke on a level so basic, so pure, response was immediate.

Matthew kissed her, his mouth hungrily tasting hers, taking and giving as she used her tongue to consume him. When he lifted his lips, she turned her head, kissed Steven, his essence and flavor just as necessary to her, just as fundamental now to her existence as his brother's.

"You've both got me so hot."

They spread her legs wider and stroked the inside of her thighs, teasing across her slit to barely brush against her clit. She cried out and chased that touch, her hips bowing off the bed.

"Mmm, you are hot. You belong to us," Steven said.

"Only ours," Matthew said.

"Yes! And you're all mine." Kelsey said

"No one else's."

"Only yours."

Kelsey rolled over, on her knees, and began to kiss her way down Matthew's chest. She paused at his nipple, bit it, then sucked the tiny nub into her mouth. He hissed his pleasure and combed his fingers though her hair so as to hang on to her, hold her.

She turned her attention to Steven, needing to taste them both, needing to taste every inch of each of them. Their flavor fed her. Their heat sustained her.

"I was so alone, just existing before you came to me."

"Not any more, baby," Steven said. "You're ours, and we take care of what's ours."

"We'll keep you warm, inside and out. You'll never be alone again," Matthew said.

These men had changed her, saved her. She was theirs, and they were hers. She needed more. One flesh.

"Please." She reached over Matthew, opened the bedside table and took out two condoms. She put one in her mouth, then tore open the other with her fingers. She stroked Matthew's cock, then slid the latex in place.

She needed them so badly she shook with it. Tossing her head to get her hair out of her way, she opened the second package, twisted her upper body, and smoothed the latex onto Steven's cock.

"Now. I can't wait. Please." She didn't wait for an answer, just straddled Matthew and took his cock deep into her cunt.

Matthew clamped his hands on her hips, held her down, and held himself deep. "Squeeze me with those marvelous muscles, Kelsey."

Kelsey flexed her pelvic floor muscles, caressing his cock with a long, slow contraction.

"Fuck, baby, I love your cunt."

Kelsey felt wicked and free. Laughing, she looked over her shoulder and gave Steven what she knew had to be the come-fuck-me look of all time.

"I need your cock in my ass, lover."

"Oh, God, yes. I want that hot little ass of yours." Steven moved, working his way behind her, finding a place for himself there. He placed a hand on each ass cheek and spread her. He reached to the bedside table for the lube. Then, he bent forward and gave her bottom hole a couple of wet, lavish licks, and applied the lube.

Then he moved again, placing his cock at her tiny pucker.

The first feel of him there made her shiver. Matthew lifted his head off the pillow and captured a nipple with his lips. Nibbling, laving, then sucking, he distracted her as his brother began to push his latex-covered cock into her.

"Baby, your ass is so tight. I don't want to hurt you," Steven said.

She felt him restraining himself. She didn't want that. She wanted his full-out passion. Matthew's, too.

"Fuck me. Take me. Hard. Fast. Deep. I need your cocks pounding into me."

"Christ." Steven pressed his cock into her, and Kelsey moved back against him, taking more of him at the same time she pressed down onto Matthew's cock.

"Yeah, that hot little pussy just got hotter and tighter." Matthew surged up into her, his hands still anchoring her hips to his.

"So tight. I've never felt anything so tight and so good." Steven pulled out a little then slid back in. He repeated those motions, solid and steady, almost exactly in sync with the way his brother fucked her cunt.

Kelsey felt on fire, desperation for more clamoring inside her. "More, damn it. Give me *more*."

The men stilled for just a moment. She'd closed her eyes, already striving for her orgasm. Now she opened them to see Matthew give Steven a look she couldn't read.

"Maybe this will help," Steven said.

Fast and hard, his open hand landed on her bare ass.

Kelsey gasped, the heat and the pain from the slap spreading through her, reaching out to tickle her clit.

"Oh, God. Yes. Do it again. *Please*."

Steven gave her two more sharp slaps as he pulled his cock nearly all the way out of her then shoved it home again. Matthew thrust up, the angle of his cock pushing him deep to her cervix, giving her another tiny bite of pain.

Kelsey cried out as her climax exploded, her entire body clenching in pleasure as wave after wave of ecstasy flooded every nerve ending, every cell. Her lovers each shouted with their own completion as they each held her tight, held her fast between them, their cocks pulsing inside her. Kelsey came and came, gushing, shivering, her keening cry of pleasure tapering to a whimper.

She welcomed Steven's weight. The sound that filled the room as they sprawled, replete, laboring for breath was fast becoming her favorite music.

Slowly, Steven lifted himself and carefully pulled his cock out of her. His hand caressed her ass. "You're nice and red here. Might hurt a little to sit in the hot tub."

"Worth it." She'd read books where men had spanked their woman, but she hadn't believed it would add anything to arousal. Now she knew better. Maybe she'd have to invest in padded panties to ease the sting of sitting. It was certainly something to think about.

Steven left the bed for the bathroom. She heard him detour to the balcony to turn on the spa.

Matthew wrapped his arms around her and slowly rolled so they were on their sides facing each other. He, too, pulled out of her carefully.

"It keeps getting better," Kelsey said. She'd been certain that this kind of wild, uninhibited sex couldn't be sustained. Yet, each time it got better, and each time she needed more.

"Easy." Steven had returned. He'd brought a warm washcloth with him and gently tended to her ass.

"You all right?" he asked her. "I didn't even stop to consider that you got banged up just the other day."

"I'm good. What about you? I didn't even stop to consider that you were shot earlier today."

"Not shot, just grazed. And I don't think I could be any better." He lay down on the bed beside her, spooning her.

Matthew quickly kissed her lips, then made his own trip to the bathroom. When he came out, he went over to the spa on the balcony and put his hand in the water.

"This is ready for us."

Kelsey got off the bed quickly, just in case Steven decided to carry her. Both men had a habit of doing so, and while she really liked that about them, she didn't want Steven to put any undue stress on his *graze*.

Kelsey eased into the water and closed her eyes. "Oh, God, that feels so good. How did I ever live without a spa?"

"I hope the spa isn't the only thing that feels that good." Matthew's voice, after-sex husky, came from her right.

"No, of course not. That bed's very nice, too."

"Smart ass," Steven said.

"It's certainly smarting at the moment," she quipped. Then she opened her eyes and looked from one to the other of her men. "It felt better tonight. Better and different."

"Because our bond is growing," Matthew said.

"Most boys' fathers tell them about the facts of life. Ours had considerably more to say," Steven said.

"When two men, or three, choose to share a woman, there's a special responsibility to ensure that the woman never feels torn, or like she's being pulled in separate directions. Dads told us that if we're the right three people, then a special bond grows between us. We all three become connected in a unique way."

"That's what I was thinking as I wanted you. That we'd be one flesh," Kelsey said.

With her lovers each holding one of her hands, Kelsey relaxed into the heat and steam, letting the spa work its magic on her. She nearly dozed, but Steven gently shook her. When she opened her eyes, she saw Matthew holding a towel out to her. She didn't think she'd been in the tub that long, but as he gathered her up and lifted her, she noticed her fingertips had wrinkled.

They dried her quickly, then tucked her into the bed. Moments later they joined her, and Kelsey found herself sliding into sleep, a lover on each side of her, snuggled close.

An hour later, the phone rang.

Chapter 21

The sign for the Triple K Diner on the state highway outside of Gatesville proclaimed it stayed open around the clock "because the trucks of America never stop." Matthew pulled Steven's Jeep into a parking spot between two semis. He'd spotted Adam's car, his own personal one and not the cruiser, and knew his best friend was already inside the diner.

He turned to look at Kelsey. "Mandy said Ginny's still inside, nursing that coffee. Temperature dipped down tonight, so she's likely hoping to stay as long as she can. She's in a booth near the back."

Kelsey nodded, then rubbed her hands together.

She'd asked to come with him. Steven had said he'd stay behind to be with Benny, no problem, as long as they let him know how things went right away. Now Matthew wondered if his woman was having second thoughts.

"You all right to do this?" Matthew asked.

"Yes. I just don't want to say the wrong thing to her."

"You won't." Matthew thought Kelsey was the perfect person to talk to Ginny Rose.

As they got out of the car, Kelsey yawned. Matthew put his arm around her and hugged her tight. "We'll go sit with her and get some coffee into you."

"At this rate," Kelsey said, "I may not be going in to my restaurant tomorrow either. Or rather, later today."

Matthew held the door for her, his eyes spotting the woman as soon as he set foot inside the long, narrow diner.

The place featured a Formica counter with stools and a row of booths along the opposite wall that was made up mostly of windows.

Adam sat at the counter nearly right across from Ginny.

Kelsey made her way down the length of the diner. She easily slipped into the booth before Ginny even looked up and noticed her.

"Oh!" The woman looked frightened when Kelsey slid over so that he could slide in beside her.

"It's all right, Ginny. Benny's safe. He's sound asleep. We just want to talk to you." Kelsey said.

Ginny looked from Kelsey to him. He'd already decided he'd stay out of it. Seeing how tired Ginny looked and how frightened just reinforced that decision. He gave her the best smile he could.

Ginny's eyes filled with tears.

"You must think I'm a terrible mother," she whispered.

"I don't," Kelsey said. She reached across the table and laid one of her hands on Ginny's. "One thing I noticed when I saw you with Benny in my restaurant was the love on your face for him."

"I was just so scared. Everything went wrong. I thought…Deke was so kind at first. I'd been alone with Benny since he was born. I worked hard, never went on welfare, you know? And I hardly ever dated. Benny's my whole world. But…but I was lonely. And Deke, he came in to the coffee shop where I worked. He seemed so nice."

Kelsey reached into her pocket and pulled out some tissues, gave them to Ginny, and then she simply let the woman talk.

Matt knew Adam could hear every word. He could tell by the hunch of his friend's shoulders that Ginny's story wasn't what Adam had expected to hear. Although his friend had said he wouldn't judge her until he'd heard what she had to say, Matt knew he had, he hadn't been able to stop himself from doing so.

Matt signaled the waitress for coffee. When the woman came over, he said, "Would you like something to eat, Ginny?"

She looked startled, as if she'd forgotten he was there. She shook her head. "Oh, no…I couldn't."

"I'll have a ham sandwich," Kelsey told the waitress. Then to Ginny she said, "I won't be able to eat the whole thing. You'll have half. All right?"

"Oh. I…yes. All right."

Kelsey fixed her coffee and waited until Ginny had put more cream into hers.

"I didn't know what else to do. Deke threatened to take his belt to Benny, and…and he hadn't even done anything! I wanted to get away from him, but he told me if I tried to leave him, I'd…I'd get worse than I was already getting. Then he told me I had to get rid of Benny. I thought…I thought if my boy was safe, then I could get away from Deke."

"Is that what you really thought?" Kelsey's voice went soft and quiet. From the corner of his eye, Matt could see Adam at the counter straining to listen.

"No." Ginny sobbed quietly, and Kelsey waited. Finally, Ginny inhaled shakily. "I was going to try to get away from him, but I thought he'd likely kill me.

"I didn't really want my baby in the system. I grew up in the system. There was one family where the missus got drunk and the mister would tell me I had to let him at me." Ginny stopped and took a sip from her coffee. The waitress returned and set the sandwich down on the table. Kelsey took half and pushed the plate over to the other woman.

Ginny never looked up, just kept her gaze focused on the table. Matt didn't think he'd ever seen a woman so broken down. At least, not since leaving Chicago. While working as a cop in the inner city, he'd seen a lot of women like Ginny, women who'd gotten themselves into bad relationships and didn't know how to get out. The men who abused these women always managed to totally short circuit their self-esteem to the point that they were truly incapable of escaping on their own.

Ginny hadn't been completely broken down because she'd gotten her son to safety, and then herself.

Ginny inhaled deeply and continued. "I didn't want that for my boy. Then I read that piece in the paper. About you and your restaurant. I cried when I read about your little boy. Then I thought you'd be good for Benny. And maybe Benny would be good for you, too. He'd be safe. And loved.

"When I woke up yesterday, I knew had to get away from Deke. I had to find my baby. I couldn't bear to be away from him another day." She cried quietly, and Kelsey said nothing, just handed her some more tissues.

Finally, she looked up and for the first time focused on Matthew. "You're the law, aren't you? You came to arrest me. I did a bad thing, leaving my boy. I deserve to go to jail. As long as my Benny's safe, that's all I care about."

Matthew wanted to assure Ginny he wasn't going to arrest her, but it really wasn't his call.

At the counter, Adam sighed heavily. He slowly turned on his stool so he faced Ginny. "No one's going to arrest you, Ms. Rose. We're not here to cause you more grief. We're here to help."

* * * *

Kelsey was glad to be back in her own kitchen.

Tracy had done a fabulous job handling things while she'd been off, and she felt better about impending vacation time when just a couple of months before, Kelsey had been certain she neither wanted nor needed to think about vacation.

Time off was all well and good, but Lusty Appetites was her baby, and she felt at her best when she was here, taking care of her business.

Kelsey laid her hand over her abdomen. Thinking of the restaurant as her baby led to other thoughts—thoughts of building families, having babies. She thought of the future for the first time in more than five years.

She couldn't deny to herself any longer that she was in love, all the way in love, with two men. Despite all the living examples here in this town, she wasn't yet one hundred percent convinced that the three of them could build a forever kind of future.

But then, life didn't come with guarantees, not ever.

Kelsey grabbed her apron and tied it on even as she heard the door to the kitchen open.

"Welcome back, boss. How do you feel? I hear you found Benny's mother," Tracy said by way of greeting.

"Thank you, fine, and yes, we found Ginny."

"I bet Benny was over the moon." Tracy set her purse in a drawer and reached for her own apron.

"He was. We weren't going to wake him last night, but he woke up as we were settling Ginny in the room next to his. I have to admit, there wasn't a dry eye in the house."

"So what happens next?"

"Adam is going to get a statement from her about Deke and likely issue an arrest warrant for assault." Kelsey could see again the bruises on the woman as she'd helped her into a large shirt to sleep in. Ginny had been too busy cuddling her son after that. She'd promised Adam she'd take a break after the lunch rush and take some photographs that could be used as evidence if he couldn't talk her into going to the clinic.

"We should find Ginny a job and a place to stay here in Lusty," Tracy said. "She'd be safe here."

Kelsey smiled. "I was thinking the same thing. Once Michelle and Carla come in, I want to have us to discuss it. Ginny has experience working in a coffee shop. I think we could use her here."

"That would be perfect. I think Michelle was talking about taking a couple of college courses come the fall," Tracy said.

"Good. Now, let's get cracking. I have a feeling there's going to be a bigger than average lunch crowd today."

Tracy nodded. "Everyone will want to make sure that you're on the mend."

Isn't that a wonderful feeling?

Kelsey couldn't remember ever being in a place where everyone would want to come out to make sure she was all right. As she began the soup and set out some beef to go in the roaster, she thought about how it seemed the entire town came together to help one small boy who wasn't even one of their own and how they'd come out for her, too.

One aspect of her future she had absolutely no doubts about was where she was going to spend the rest of her life. Nothing would ever lure her away from Lusty, Texas.

Chatter from the dining room told her that Michelle and Carla had arrived for work.

"Hey, boss. Good to have you back! Are you all right? I hear you found Benny's mom!"

Kelsey smiled and let Tracy fill them in. The waitresses stashed their purses and washed up, then grabbed aprons to give a hand with some of the minor kitchen duties.

"I helped Morgan with the canvass yesterday," Michelle said. "We found out that several people saw the same car in town just before the shooting. We don't think much, usually, about strange cars in town. But there was only one, a dark blue Pontiac. No one got a license number, but the man behind the wheel was a big bruiser. That's what Aunt Anna said."

"Maybe it's enough information that Adam can get a lead." At least Kelsey hoped it was enough information. Matthew hadn't pressed her this morning, but there was still the matter of her making a decision about seeing a hypnotist.

If she could avoid it, she would. She really didn't understand all that would be involved, but she knew one thing for certain. She didn't really want to remember anything more about that horrible day.

The memories she already had would be with her for the rest of her life.

"Anyway," Michelle continued, "I was kind of nervous at first because I was afraid that people would have said they'd seen a silver Prius, but no one reported seeing one of those. And that Austin hottie who comes here a couple times a week certainly couldn't ever be called a bruiser."

"The Austin hottie?" Kelsey asked.

"Yeah, you know the one I pointed out to you? He has a crush on you."

Kelsey vaguely recalled the man. Dark hair, moustache, and carrying a few extra pounds, though not in his face. He'd come to try the cuisine, he'd told her, because of that write-up in the Waco paper.

Note to self, avoid being the subject of any future newspaper interviews.

So far that one had netted her more business but also seemed to be the catalyst for some not-so-pleasant experiences.

Although, in all honesty, since that article had been the impetus for getting Ginny Rose out of a dangerous situation, she guessed it wasn't all bad.

Still, she wouldn't call that new customer a hottie. In fact, when he looked at her, she kind of got the creeps.

"Did you get his name yet?" Tracy asked.

"I was going to ask him on Sunday. Then we had all that excitement about little Benny, and the next thing I knew, he was gone. If he shows up today, you can be sure I'll worm it out of him. I mean, he does have a crush on Kelsey, but I think he likes me, too. Once he figures out Kelsey doesn't even see him, the field will be all mine."

Tracy and Carla laughed. Kelsey just shook her head.

"What makes you think he has a crush on me?" Kelsey asked.

"Well, for one thing, he's asked a ton of questions about you. And then, every time you come into the dining room, he can't take his eyes off you. His face gets all serious, you know, like he doesn't want to miss a single moment of your presence."

Kelsey felt her face heat, but at the same time a sense of discomfort washed through her. "Well, you're right, of course. I don't see him." Then, because they were all looking at her avidly, she added, "I've got my hands full with the brothers Benedict."

Since her staff was all present, she told them a little about Ginny and suggested that she might find employment with them at Lusty Appetites.

"That's perfect! I was worried about leaving you short in the fall," Michelle said. "Now I don't have to worry."

"Great. I'll wait a couple of days to ask her if she'd be interested. She needs a bit of time to get her wind back."

"I knew a woman when I lived in Philadelphia," Carla said. "She didn't get knocked around physically, but emotionally. Takes time to feel whole again."

"I hope she decides to stay here in Lusty," Kelsey said. "She'll be able to feel whole again here."

They all got busy, the waitresses checking to make sure the dining room was ready, and she and Tracy getting down to the serious business of getting ready to feed the town.

Before she knew it, the doors were open and people started flowing in for lunch. Mindful of good PR, but mostly because she loved this town and its people, Kelsey made certain to take several tours of the dining room.

By one, when the lunch crowd began to taper, she had healthy receipts and an overflow of flowers and well wishes to show for the day.

"I'm going to take a break," she announced to her staff. "I should be back in an hour. If you need me—"

"We'll just call down to the sheriff's office," Tracy said.

Kelsey shook her head at the silly grins facing her. She guessed there were no secrets in a small town, especially in a small town like Lusty.

Her men had asked her not to go anywhere alone, but it was a short walk to the sheriff's office, which was right in the middle of downtown Lusty. The late summer sun burned down without the relief of a single cloud.

As she waited for the traffic light, the sound of a car's engine caught her attention. The glint of sun on silver flashed in the corner of her eye and made her turn and look.

The late model Prius gleamed brightly, looking chic and expensive. Which made the sight of the driver, holding a handgun pointed at her, seem totally out of place.

"Get into the car, Ms. Madison. You and I have some unfinished business."

Chapter 22

"How'd it go with Ginny?" Matthew asked the moment Adam came into the office. He'd felt too involved to handle the interview in his official capacity as deputy. Adam hadn't minded doing it instead. Matthew knew his own emotions had become involved because he loved Benny. He also loved their woman, and she'd made her feelings on the subject of Ginny Rose very clear.

Matthew thought their Kelsey was one hell of a generous woman.

"I have Ginny talked into pressing charges against Deke. She's scared, and I find I really can't blame her. She knows she has to do something or else everything she went through these last few days will have been for nothing."

Matthew stayed quiet then because he knew his best friend well. Adam was coldly furious and dealing with it in his own way. He'd only seen him this angry once before, but the memory hadn't diminished in all the years since that incident. He hadn't been sheriff then, but a college junior who'd come across some men who'd been forcing themselves on a young woman. There'd been three of them, and Adam had lit into them all before Matt had a chance to join him.

Adam reached the corner of his desk and just stood there, looking down at it. In the next instant, he grabbed his coffee cup, spun around, and hurled it against the far wall.

The china mug shattered into a thousand pieces, the crash of pottery against brick an eloquent scream of rage.

"She let me stay with her while Uncle James examined her at the clinic. We had taken pictures to document the evidence. Deke had used his belt on her the night she left Benny. She's covered in welts."

"Jesus Christ." Matthew had suspected something because the woman had moved stiffly, and she hadn't wanted to let him near her. He was rather surprised she'd allowed Adam that close. Then again, most women recognized the caretaker in Adam.

"Kelsey's going to try and talk her into staying in Lusty," Matthew said. "She's going to offer her a job. We'll get her a place to live, too. We'll all take care of her from now on."

Adam inhaled deeply, then let it out. "Good. Your instincts were right about Ginny. I should have listened to you. I'm sorry."

"You did listen. That's why you were at the diner, out of uniform."

The phone rang and Matthew answered it. "Lusty Sheriff's Department. Hi, Burgess. Any luck with those tapes? Oh yeah? Great. I don't suppose you got the license plate?" Matthew listened for a moment then frowned. "Yeah, a bit too much to hope for. Still, I'm glad we've got the guy going *and* coming. Send it to my e-mail. Thanks."

He hung up the phone and looked over at Adam.

"That was Burgess with the Waco P. D. They've finished scanning the surveillance tapes taken at the mall the day Kelsey was attacked. They show the Taurus arriving at the mall, a female driver getting out, and just a few minutes later, a man getting out of a silver Prius and boosting the Taurus. No clear image of the man and none of the Prius' plates at that point. And then, several hours later, they show our perp getting out of the Taurus where he dumped it at the commercial unloading area. This one gives us a clear shot of him. Burgess is sending the footage as an e-mail attachment."

"Good. Maybe I can take my frustration out on that s.o.b. when we catch him."

The door to the office burst open, and Michelle rushed in. Nearly hysterical, she grabbed Matthew by his shirt. "Oh, God. Oh, God. He has her. Do something. He has her!"

* * * *

"Who are you? What do you want?" Kelsey had never been so terrified. The sight of the gun had momentarily overwhelmed everything and she'd gotten into his car, unable to do anything else.

Slowly, Kelsey's mind cleared. The man drove and kept the gun pointed at her as he followed the route out of town, the route that would take them past where he'd rammed her off the road last Sunday.

"You can call me Con. You really don't know, do you? That's a shame. I couldn't take the chance that you'd remember me. You might have. Yeah, you probably would have as soon as my mug started getting flashed all over television screens across the state."

"I don't know what you're talking about!"

"I was there that day. The day Jimmy whacked your old man and your kid. He was just supposed to rush in, grab the cash, and get out. Clean and fast. Nobody was supposed to die. Little prick. It wasn't my fault he was all hopped up on drugs. I was glad when I heard he'd been killed by the cops resisting arrest. No trial and no dropping a dime on me."

Kelsey looked at the man, the one Michelle had dubbed Mr. Hottie. He looked different without that extra weight he'd been carrying. She studied him but didn't find anything else familiar about him.

Apparently, he didn't care for her scrutiny. He waved his gun at her and screamed, "You sat in your fucking car and stared right at me, bitch. Don't tell me you didn't see me!"

But she hadn't. A dam broke in her mind, and images came flooding back.

They'd fought that morning. Kelsey had found a note in one of Philip's pockets the week before, a woman's name and a phone number. She'd believed him when he'd told her it was a business acquaintance, just someone he had to call to set up a meeting with.

Except the doubts had been there, fed by small clues and changes in his behavior, and the doubts wouldn't go away. He'd come home late the night before, very late, and while she'd waited for him, while she'd worried that maybe he'd been in an accident, she'd used her computer to check out the name and the number.

Doing a reverse phone number search, she'd learned the number connected not to a business address, but a private one. Marissa Lane. Paying the fee the website charged for extra information, she discovered his business contact worked as a waitress at a bar near his office.

So they'd fought, and he'd told her the truth. And he'd excused his behavior by saying it had only happened a couple of times. That it was only physical. That it never would have happened in the first place if Kelsey would just try to be a little sexier. That it was all Kelsey's fault he wasn't fulfilled as a man.

They were expected at a friend's for the day. She didn't want to go, but Philip insisted they keep their word and go. When he stopped at the convenience store, she'd been so mad, she could barely see straight. She'd been so mad, she'd been thinking about asking for a divorce. Until a man's shout had pulled her out of fury and gunshots had thrown her into terror and grief.

Kelsey came back to the present, the flashback so fast, so sharp, it felt surreal. This man, Con, had been nowhere in that flashback. She'd been lost in her thoughts and her anger, her gaze on her husband when those gun shots had exploded. Philip had died, and in the aftermath, she'd forgotten that the last words between them had been angry words. Her subconscious had buried that, until now.

"I've straightened out my life since then. I've done everything right. I even got married. " Con continued on his rant, his voice rising, sounding more manic with each word. "I'm going to get into politics. And then there was that picture of you in the paper. Seriously, I'd thought they'd sent you to the nut house. You fucking lost it. I thought you were tucked away in crazy land. Then I see you aren't. If you hadn't let them do that article on you, this wouldn't be happening. I'm entitled to live my life. It's all your fault that I have to do this."

Kelsey thought of Matthew and Steven and the life they could have together, the life they would have together. She thought of Ginny, who gave up her son rather than risk him near a man who'd been turning more and more violent.

And she thought about this jerk waving his gun, another loser telling her it wasn't his fault, that somehow she was responsible for his mistakes. This jerk belonged to the past, and she was, by God, done with the past.

Up ahead the road curved, a long sweeping S-bend to the left. Beyond that, she knew, lay a slight rise, a small hill before a long, straight stretch. It was just there where he'd forced her off the road last Sunday.

Kelsey didn't let herself think as her anger rose up, white hot, blinding. The gun swept the air in front of her face back, then forth as Con tried to focus on driving and keeping the weapon pointed at her.

As soon as they crested the hill, Kelsey screamed and grabbed the hand with the gun in both of hers, slamming it hard against the dash over and over again.

"You crazy fucking bitch! Let go!"

He tried to fight her and the car. Kelsey didn't let up, just kept banging his wrist against the dash.

The gun exploded, loud, sudden. The force of the recoil threw Kelsey against her seat and the gun into the back seat. The windshield shattered. Kelsey had turned her head but felt but felt sharp prickles on the side of her face.

Con screamed. "My eyes! My eyes!" Both hands covered his face.

Kelsey grabbed the steering wheel at the same time she shoved her foot down between Con's legs and stomped down on the brake.

The car had nearly stopped when she turned the key off, grabbed it from the ignition, and threw it out through the hole where the windshield had been. It skittered off the hood.

Her fingers shook as she unfastened her seatbelt and got out of the car and ran. Her ears were still ringing from the gunshot when Steven's Jeep roared up over the hill.

* * * *

She'd been crying and her face was dotted with blood, and he'd never seen anyone more beautiful in all his life.

He stood close to her while Uncle James assessed Kelsey's injuries.

"I'm getting a little tired of seeing you in my clinic, young lady," Dr. James said.

"I'm a little tired of seeing you, too," Kelsey replied.

They both grinned.

Steven stood to the left of Kelsey, her hand folded into his, as Dr. James continued to apply ointment to the tiny cuts on the right side of her face.

Because he couldn't resist, Steven leaned over and kissed the side of her face gently.

The door to the exam room burst open, and Matthew barreled through the door. His eyes swept her, head to toe.

"I'm okay, sweetheart," Kelsey said.

"You're a crazy woman," Matthew asserted. He all but pushed Dr. James out of the way so that he could give her a hard, fast kiss. "And when we get home I'm seriously considering putting you across my knee and walloping your ass until it's even redder than it was the other night. We told you to stay at the restaurant until one of us came to get you!" Then he stepped back and turned to Steven. "Did she tell you what she did to escape?"

Steven felt his blood run cold as Matthew relayed how Kelsey had escaped from an armed gunman.

"My God," Steven said. "You *are* a crazy woman, and a walloping definitely sounds right."

It didn't appear their assessments or threats fazed her in the slightest. "But you guys still love me anyway, right?"

"Hell, yes." Steven's fervent declaration was echoed by his brother.

"I didn't remember him," Kelsey said as the doctor continued to work on her. "I finally remembered the rest of that day, which I've never done. Philip and I had fought. I was so angry my mind was full of our argument. I...I was considering divorce. I truly never even noticed that man."

"His name is Wesley Connors, a Realtor from Austin, and erstwhile mayoral candidate," Matthew said. "Needless to say, he won't get elected now. Adam went with him to the hospital in Waco. He got quite a bit more glass in the face than you did. He claims it wasn't him who fired that sniper rifle at the two of you the other day. He's trying to cut a deal. I hope to hell he fails, but I don't hold out much hope. He claims he can give the D.A. a really powerful and important man." Matthew sighed. "We'll see."

"The good news is she's not badly injured," Dr. James said. "I'll give you a prescription for some antibiotic cream to apply twice a day for a couple of days. I don't think she'll scar too badly."

"The only thing we care about is that she's safe and sound," Steven said.

"Damn right," Matthew said.

"Well, then." Dr. James put both hands on Kelsey's shoulders and gave her a good stare. "You, young lady, stay out of trouble."

"Yes, sir."

Steven found himself returning Matthew's grin. How many times had they each answered one or the other of the Doctors Jessop just that way?

Dr. James leaned forward and kissed her forehead. Then he nodded to Steven and Matt and left the room.

Steven stroked a hand gently down Kelsey's hair, so damn glad that he could, that she was here and alive and safe. "Does it hurt, sweetheart?"

"Just a little. The worst part was the gun going off. My ears just stopped ringing."

"You're lucky that's all it did. When I think—*Jesus.*" Matthew choked that out, then stepped forward and wrapped his arms around their woman.

When Matthew eased his hug, she turned her gaze to Steven. "How did you know where to find me and get to me so fast?" She didn't have to explain herself.

"I had the sudden urge to go to town and was just pulling up at the sheriff's office when Matt and Adam came racing out, heading for their cars. Matt shouted to me that your attacker had you. The first place I thought to go was where that bastard had run you off the road on Sunday. I just floored it. I didn't even look to see if the light was green or not."

"Thank you. I wasn't certain if maybe Connors wouldn't somehow find that damn gun and start shooting at me even as I was running away from him. I could barely see anything I was so scared. So I just ran."

"Jesus, Kelsey, you don't have to thank me. You're my heart. I couldn't bear it if anything happened to you," Steven said. He couldn't stop the shiver that ran down his spine.

"It's over." Kelsey stretched up to kiss Matthew, and then she pulled Steven closer and kissed him, too. "It's over, and I just want to go home. I want to soak in the hot tub, maybe sip some wine." She blushed, looked down, then back up, meeting first Steven's gaze and then Matt's. "I got hot when you said you were going to spank me."

Steven laughed, relief rolling through him. "Good thing," he said, "because I have a feeling that may be a regular activity for us."

"If I like it as much as I think I do, you can count on it," Kelsey said. "So, can we go home, now?"

"Yeah," Matthew said. "Adam will come out tomorrow to take your statement. For now, we can head out."

"Of course, there is that crowd in the waiting room to be got through," Steven said as he helped her off the exam table.

"Crowd?" Kelsey narrowed her eyes. "What kind of crowd?"

"Oh, just the usual," Steven said. "You've got your Benedicts and your Kendalls and your Jessops, your Jessop-Kendalls, and Parkers, and Joneses—"

"And Parker-Joneses," Kelsey finished for him. "In other words, family."

"Yeah. One thing about this town," Matthew said, "it's lousy with family."

"Nothing lousy about that," Kelsey countered.

Steven's heart had tripped when Kelsey had said "family," and he knew from the glitter in Matthew's eyes that he felt the same.

"So yes, we'll go home," Steven said, "and talk about family."

"There's nothing I'd rather do," Kelsey said.

Chapter 23

They didn't let go of her hands the entire time they'd walked from clinic to the car.

As predicted, the waiting room was full of family. Bernice hugged her first, sniffing back her tears, then turned Kelsey over to her two husbands. Jonathan and Caleb hugged her, then passed her off to Adam's parents, and so it went.

When she saw Michelle, Kelsey held her close. "If you hadn't stepped outside when you did and then gotten help, I don't know if I could have gotten away from that bastard. He might have still been able to get to his gun and kill me."

"I feel so bad that I thought he was a hottie," Michelle sniffed.

"Don't. He played that role on purpose," Matthew said.

Eventually they made their way through the crowd and outside to Steven's Jeep. Much as they had that first night they'd picked her up, they all three sat in the front. Matthew held her tight on his lap as Steven made quick work of the drive home.

Ginny and Benny were snuggled together in Ginny's bed, indulging in an afternoon nap. They crept past her room to the sanctuary of the master bedroom.

Kelsey had been aware of a fine tremor running through Matthew's body as she'd sat on his lap. Once the door closed behind them, she threw her arms around him, sensing he needed to hold her tight.

"Scared the living hell out of us, baby," Matthew said.

"Scared the living hell out of me, too." Kelsey had been able to hold on to her tears all through the ordeal of overpowering Connors, of being treated at the clinic. Now, she couldn't hold on anymore.

Sobs racked her. Steven stepped close, and the two men enveloped her completely with their bodies and their love.

"Adrenaline crash," Matthew said.

"Yeah," Steven agreed.

They held her until the storm lessened and then they began to undress her. She reached for the buttons of their shirts, but they both batted her hands away, shucking their clothes quickly. When they stepped back to her, she dropped to her knees.

Two big, beautiful, hard cocks bobbed, waiting for her attention. She loved these men so much. She wanted nothing more than to pleasure them. She filled her hands with them, squeezing and stroking their cocks in a languid rhythm.

She took Matthew into her mouth, sucking deep. A masculine hiss of pleasure and the firm threading of fingers through her hair rewarded her efforts. She pulled her mouth off Matthew, turned her head, and sucked Steven's cock into her mouth.

She loved the taste of both of them, marveling that she could tell the difference, their flavors subtly and uniquely their own.

Steven's hand joined his brother's in caressing her hair, and Kelsey pleased herself by lavishing this form of loving on her men by turn.

"Your mouth is fucking *wonderful*," Steven groaned.

"It is," Matthew said.

Kelsey hummed along Steven's shaft, her tongue stroking as she raised and lowered her head over him, then increasing the pressure of the suction she used until he groaned again and thrust his hips.

She slid off his cock with a slurp and then took Matthew again, treating him to the same slow, wet loving. She had to flex her pussy when her moisture ran so fast she thought her thighs would be covered.

"Enough. Our turn." Matthew said.

Kelsey sat back, gazing up at her impassioned lovers, but before she could ask what they intended, Steven picked her up and laid her on the bed. Kelsey giggled when they both dove for her.

"Hold on to the headboard and don't let go," Matthew said.

Something about that commanding tone of his could light her fire almost as much as any touch. Complying, needing to just give them whatever they needed or wanted, Kelsey wrapped her hands around the brass rails.

"Your cocks feel better in my hands than this cold metal does."

"Glad to hear it. Now give me your nectar," Steven said as he buried his face in her cunt.

Kelsey groaned, her arousal shooting sharp and high. She arched her hips to press her pussy against Steven's avid mouth. Matthew caressed her hair, gently turning her head to him.

His mouth took hers in a kiss more carnal, more feral than any she'd tasted. His mouth demanded surrender, submission, and Kelsey was helpless to refuse him.

He ran his hand over her breasts, his touch possessive and obsessive. He pulled his lips from hers.

"Ours," Matthew said, his voice raw and his face fierce. Kelsey knew here came the primitive, the one the best of men held in check until that moment when emergence became unstoppable.

Steven inserted two fingers into her cunt, rubbing them back and forth over her G-spot while his tongue lapped her folds. "Ours," Steven said.

Two lovers, two demanding male gazes, but one love. One love and one future.

"Yes. Yours. Only yours."

Steven sucked her clit into his mouth at the same instant Matthew lowered his lips to a nipple, nipped, and then sucked it deep.

Kelsey screamed as she came, the orgasm rising up like a tsunami, totally unexpected, totally overpowering. Her hips bucked, but her men held her fast so that she had no choice but to take the ecstasy they gave her.

"Oh, God." She fought for breath, fought for strength, her breasts petted gently by Matthew as Steven placed sweet kisses on her thighs.

And then the brothers swapped positions.

"You have a juicy cunt," Steven whispered as he snuggled close to her. "Taste."

She tasted herself and Steven, and the combined flavor rekindled her arousal. His lips and tongue devoured her, giving and taking, and Kelsey reached up with one hand, her fingers combing through his hair, then holding him hard.

Matthew traced his finger over her pussy, then settled his open mouth there. He turned his head back and forth, and the erotic friction made her shiver with need. Kelsey lifted her hips to chase his oral possession and lifted her breasts when Steven began to caress and pinch.

"I love you, Kelsey. Now and forever," Steven said.

"That's what we want, sweetheart." Matthew lifted his head, his gaze piercing hers. "We want forever. Forever and children, and someday, grandchildren."

"I love you both. I love you so much."

"Then say yes," Matthew said. "Say yes so we can be naked inside you. We want to give you our child."

Those words melted her heart and heated her blood. She never thought she'd ever want that again. She'd surrendered that dream to cruel fate. These men had changed her mind. Their love had healed her heart, and while she knew there would always be a piece of that heart missing, the rest would be strong, and full, and treasured.

"Yes. Yes, please."

Steven reached down and gently pulled her right leg higher, spreading her even wider. He bent down, kissed her gently, then turned his gaze on his brother.

Matthew surged up her body and thrust his cock into her. He held himself over her, his eyes closed as if savoring the sensation of being so deep inside her.

"Your cunt is hot and tight. It feels like home."

She felt each ripple, each thrust, the heat within her incredible. She wrapped her legs around Matthew, pulling him tighter on each thrust, lifting into him to consume as much of him as she could. The slap of his balls against her ass fed the flames of her passion.

Steven kissed her again, lightly, then leaned back, away, giving her completely to his brother.

Matthew wrapped his arms around her and laid his mouth on hers. How exciting to receive his cock and his tongue at the same time in the same demanding, commanding cadence. The friction of his pubic hair against her clit sent a tingling shimmer throughout her body.

"I want to come." Wrapping herself around him, she said, "Come inside me. Give me your child."

"Yes." As his words had done for her, so hers inflamed him. She saw that by the fierce rapture sweeping his face.

The instant she felt the first spurt of his semen within her she exploded in orgasm, the spasms so sweet, so exciting, she grabbed him tighter and rubbed herself against him as a keening mew rose up from her soul.

The waves buffeted her, and each convulsion of Matthew's cock within her took her higher and higher still even as the orgasm began to ebb.

Matthew rested his forehead on hers, his breathing fast and harsh. Holding his weight on his arms, his chest just brushing against hers.

"More, oh, God, I need *more*." Desperation like she'd never known swamped her. She'd just come twice, but it felt as though she'd not had an orgasm in years, decades. She hovered so close, so close, but the sensations felt suspended, just out of reach, and she shook with need.

"Here." Matthew slid out of her and rolled to the left, making room for his brother. Steven moved quickly, coming down between her spread thighs, then plunged his cock into her.

"Oh, yes, so hot and tight and *good*." Steven might have been speaking for her, too, because his sentiments so perfectly matched her own.

She grabbed on to him, twined her legs around his hips, and pushed up and into him with each of his thrusts. "Fuck me. Come inside me. Make me pregnant." Her arousal kept climbing and climbing, soaring higher and higher until she thought she'd never reach the pinnacle, never come. "Oh, God, I need more!"

"Yeah," Matthew said. "Flip her."

Kelsey gasped as Steven wrapped his arms around her and rolled so that she straddled him. Oh, God, that felt so much better. But it wasn't enough. She began to ride him. The sounds of a drawer opening just barely registered.

"Kiss me," Steven said. "Kiss me while I fill you."

His mouth took hers, a ravenous plunder that demanded all and gave everything. Behind her, she felt Matthew move close, then the cool glide of lube coating her anus.

"Take us both, Kelsey. Fuck us both at the same time while we make our baby."

Matthew leaned into her, his cock opening her rosebud, pushing hard, pushing deep. Kelsey groaned, everything in her tightening, the slight pain of Matthew's invasion adding to the thrill of need and arousal clawing at her.

"God, yes. So much tighter. I'm going to come in you, Kelsey," Steven said.

Matthew began to thrust, his strokes matching his brother's. Steven held her close as Matthew pressed down on her back so she could no longer control the motions. Matthew's low growl told her he was already close to coming.

"Now!" Steven said.

Deep inside her body, she felt his cock surge, felt the spasm and then the hot stream of his seed hitting her cervix at the same time she felt Matthew push deep and erupt inside her ass.

Her orgasm broke, the climax so fierce it set her entire body ablaze with bliss, a shivering, quivering coming of such magnitude she thought the house must be shaking with it.

Steven and Matthew both shouted their completion, holding themselves tight inside her, and it was enough, that pulsing of their ejaculations proved enough to keep her coming and coming.

She collapsed on Steven and had to blink because she could see spots and needed to get her focus back.

"Holy hell, I'm wrecked." Steven's words puffed against her neck. Kelsey laughed.

Matthew, lying on her back but not too heavily, said, "Pretty powerful stuff when you decide to make a baby."

Matthew pulled out of her carefully and then helped her off Steven. He got off the bed, returning moments later with a warm, wet cloth. He tended her, stroking a hand down her back.

Afterwards, Kelsey rolled onto her back, and Matthew stretched out beside her so she was once more in the middle.

"Will you marry us, sweetheart? We were meant to be together," Matthew said.

"Yes," Steven said. "We were meant to be together. Marry us, please."

Kelsey looked from one to the other. "How is that done, exactly?"

"The Benedict way," Steven said.

"Isn't everything?" Kelsey asked. She hoped her smile told them she was teasing.

"Of course," Matthew said.

Kelsey thought he sounded rather smug about that.

"You'll be legally married to Matthew," Steven said, "because he's the oldest of the two of us. That can be done anywhere. But then there'll be a family ceremony, where we'll speak vows and pledge ourselves to each other. That will be our real wedding ceremony."

Kelsey smiled. "The Benedict way. I like the sound of that." She lay content between her two future husbands.

"You are the heart of us, of our family," Matthew said. "Knowing that you love us both, that we're a unit, together—hell, it's the greatest feeling in the world. We'd do anything for you. Never doubt it."

"I told myself that it would only be physical between us," Kelsey said, "and I used the excuse of the shooting. And while that was a part of it, the biggest part was what happened just *before* the shooting. I'd suppressed it, I guess. But when Connors was holding the gun on me, telling me it was *my fault* he had to kill me, it brought back the fight Philip and I had. I'd caught him cheating on me, you see."

"And he blamed *you* for his infidelity?" Steven asked incredulously.

"Yes, and a part of me believed it. That's natural, I think. And why I really didn't want to get involved, seriously, again. Because I'd never resolved that."

"You'll never have to worry about either of us cheating on you," Matthew said.

"Absolutely not. That's not the Benedict way," Steven confirmed.

Kelsey grinned. "Well, you sure as hell won't ever have to worry about me, either. I've found love under two Benedicts. Once you have the best, you don't have to look any further."

"Oh, darlin', we're not worried about that even one little bit," Matthew said.

"We're going to keep you so busy and so exhausted you'll never even know there *are* other men."

"Pretty big words there, cowboy. Why don't you show me?" Kelsey said.

"Why don't we both show you?" Steven said.

Kelsey shrieked with laugher when Steven jumped up, scooped her into his arms and headed, with Matthew right beside them, for the hot tub.

THE END

Siren Publishing, Inc.
www.SirenPublishing.com

LaVergne, TN USA
27 November 2010
206474LV00010B/45/P